JUGGLING WITH TURNIPS

First published in 2018
by Eyewear Publishing Ltd
Suite 333, 19-21 Crawford Street
London, W1H 1PJ
United Kingdom

Graphic design by Edwin Smet
Cover photograph by Gunther Kleinert, Getty images
Author photograph by Bernard Walsh

Printed in England by TJ International Ltd, Padstow, Cornwall

Set in Bembo 13 / 17 pt
ISBN 978-1-912477-62-3

WWW.EYEWEARPUBLISHING.COM

Juggling With Turnips

Karl MacDermott

EYEWEAR PUBLISHING

For Charlie
and Phil

Contents

MEETING WITH SISYPHUS

'Karl.'

'Sisyphus. Thanks for seeing me.'

'Why wouldn't I find time to see you? Sure, aren't you one of SOS Management's oldest clients?'

'1997.'

'Where does the time go? So what's the idea?'

'I'm working on a book of short stories, short fiction... well, vignettes.'

'Hold it. Short stories are awful difficult to sell this weather. No one reads that kind of stuff anymore, what with the internet and all that carry on. Novels are struggling as well. Basically no one reads, like. So that's a problem for people who write.'

'Yeh. I just try and keep doing the work, so eh, bear with me, Sisyphus. I've called the collection *Snapshots of Inconsequence*.'

'Snapshots of what? Ah, for fuck sake, Karl. That's not a great title, to be honest.'

'I've brought the first three stories in with me. Would you like to read them?'

'Sure. Sure. Yeh. Yeh. Leave them on the desk. I'll do that later.'

'Promise?'

'Did you ever think of thinking outside the box, Karl, as the Americans say?'

'What does that even mean, Sisyphus? Thinking outside the box. Have you ever known anyone having to think *inside* a box apart from Harry Houdini?'

'Alright. Alright. Now, look I was thinking, maybe you should write a memoir.'

'A memoir?'

'Readers love memoirs. You know, Fidelma, my partner, she has contacts in Sludge Lagoon Press, and they say nothing sells like a good memoir.'

'But you need to be famous. My profile would be, uh, excruciatingly modest.'

'Stop it. Didn't you win that Nora Barnacle Anything To Do With Galway Literary Award a few years ago?'

'2001.'

'Ok. So you're not permanently in the public eye. Or intermittently, even. But that doesn't matter. All we have to do with this memoir thing is find an angle.'

'What do you mean?'

'Now I'm just putting this out there. You weren't ever abused as a child?'

'No.'

'That always works. Readers love that stuff. No priest ever messed with you?'

'No.'

'Did you ever have a drink problem?'

'No. I'm a very moderate drinker. I was once described by a friend as a clean-living Bukowski.'

'The *Barfly* fella?'

'Yeh.'

'Gotcha. Drugs?'

'No. I mean, I've had the odd spliff in college but...'

'Jays, what'll we do with you at all? What about cancer? My cancer hell! Testicular cancer always works for the auld men. Publishers can't get enough of it. For the auld women it would be the auld breast cancer. And did they get the one or both removed. That always gets them in the news, or if they say they've had an abortion fifteen years ago, that always gets them on the telly. But you wouldn't have had an abortion, you'd have to be a woman for that.'

'I think that would be a prerequisite.'

'You've never felt like a woman, have you? You're not like gender confused, or something like? That would be great if you were, it's really in at the minute.'

'No. I'm a man. My gender isn't flowing. Fluid. Whatever.'

'Oh. Pity. You're not gay like? Are you? Although the auld gay thing seems a bit passé at this stage. You didn't grow up gay in Galway and have a tormented secret double life?'

'No. I was more like a closet heterosexual.'

'Uh?'

'I took my time. Nothing much happened to me when I was growing up. I had more of an unspent youth than a misspent youth. Sour sixteen. Not sweet.'

'Ah, for fuck's sake. Not even any hair-raising escapades then.'

'Not really. Oh, wait a minute. I raided an orchard once with a bunch of older boys. This guy Colin came up to me one day after school and said 'Hey, do you want to come along and raid an orchard tonight?' And I thought, to raid an orchard! It sounds so exciting. All these images streamed into my head. Scaling walls. Searchlights. Ropes. Guard-dogs. And of course, apples. But at the end of the day, when we got round to it, all there was, was just the apples. And they were so bitter, we couldn't even eat them. Life can be so disappointing.'

'Arey, what'll we do with you, at all.'

'I think raiding that orchard was the first of my 'is that all there is' moments.'

'What?'

'You know from that Peggy Lee song, 'Is That All There Is?'

'Jesus! Peggy Lee. Houdini. The trouble with you, Karl, is you're living in the past. Your head is pointed in the wrong direction. It's the future you have to think of.'

'Sorry Sisyphus. Maybe I'm just a bit depressed.'

'What?'

'I don't know. Maybe I'm just a bit depressed.'

'Hang on. Are you serious about the auld depression? That would be great! A mental health angle for a memoir. Always works. Manna from heaven. Listen, have you ever had suicidal thoughts? Tell me you've had suicidal thoughts. That's the biggie! Suicidal thoughts! Did he want to do himself in? How close was he to doing himself in! Jays, they lap that up.'

'Well, I'm not *that* depressed.'

'That would have been too good. Are you on medication?'

'No. I'm just a bit down all the time.'

'Arey, that's fuckin' useless.'

'I get headaches. Chronic tension headaches.'

'Arey, will you fuck off! Everyone gets fuckin' headaches. *You're* giving me a headache. Do you do mindfulness? For your auld depression and headaches. They fuckin' love mindfulness. It's one of those zeitgeisty things.'

'No.'

'Do you want to try it? And then write a book about it. *Me and My Mindfulness*.'

'*Me and My Mindfulness*?! Come on, Sisyphus. I consider myself an architect of the imagination. I do not write self-help books!'

'All right, look, it was just a suggestion. Listen, I'm running a bit behind schedule, think we'll have to wrap it up for today. Have a think about some of those things we've discussed. I'll try and read these three stories anyway at some stage and I'll get back to you soon. Alright. Keep the flag flying, Karl, keep it flying. I'll be seeing you.'

THE THREE STORIES SISYPHUS WAS MEANT TO READ

A SERIES OF DIM

By the turn of the 21st century, Cosmo Kincaid had stopped drinking with other men in bars to avoid the embarrassment of having to urinate side by side with an acquaintance. It was not that he had a particularly small penis, although it was 'nothing to write home about' as his first and only serious girlfriend Doreen had confided to a mutual friend in the summer of 1989.

What also had to be factored into these situations was the possibility of being caught in the crossfire of urine spray. Someone else's urine spray. Cosmo, himself, was not a powerful micturator. He had a tentative sphincter muscle that automatically tightened any time he was forced to engage in a strained conversation with some young bucko, hands on hips, proudly watching his Thomas the Tank Engine create a powerful deluge. A deluge that inadvertently led to stains. On other people's clothing.

Cosmo always preferred going to the cubicle. It was safer there. No strangers (or acquaintances). He could relax. Although, once back in 1998, he got a dreadful fright when he looked up and saw an extremely tall man – must have been nearly seven-foot – looking down on him from the cubicle next door. Won't happen again, he thought. Abnormally tall people don't live long.

'What took you so long?'

Phyllis Bourke, Cosmo's (non-male) drinking companion, welcomed him back to their table.

'Had to wait for a cubicle to be free.'

Cosmo sat down and sighed.

'You know you are getting old when you can no longer read the graffiti on toilet walls.'

Phyllis sipped her drink.

'Or write graffiti on toilet walls.'

Cosmo looked at Phyllis.

'You've written graffiti on toilet walls?'

'In my time.'

Cosmo was intrigued.

'I always wondered about that. Do you have to plan to write graffiti on a toilet wall? Do you already bring your marker pen with you when you go out that evening? Or do you just happen to have a marker pen in your pocket while in the cubicle?'

'Whatever takes your fancy. Sometimes, I've even borrowed a marker from the barman.'

'So, you've gone up to a barman and said, 'Can I borrow your marker pen? I want to deface your property.' '

Phyllis looked at Cosmo.

'You know the trouble with you, Cosmo. You are

too repressed. You should try and live a little.'

'What, by writing obscenities on some toilet wall?'

'Dare you.'

That night Cosmo ruminated on what Phyllis had said. Maybe she was right. He was inhibited. His name, Cosmo Kincaid, suggested an extra-terrestrial cowboy with superpowers, but his reality, twenty-five years working in the accounts department of Baileys & Flagstaff, was different. Names can be so misleading. Nina Simone was christened Eunice.

Next day at work, as he computed some projected sales figures, he thought once more about Phyllis's comment. Suddenly on impulse, he grabbed hold of the new Primo Jet Super black marker lying on his desk, got up and strode purposefully into the Baileys & Flagstaff toilet cubicle. While in there, he crouched and wrote a small x on the white wall. He felt energized and excited, but when he tried to wipe it away immediately (old hesitant Cosmo) it morphed into a swastika. His panic and guilt only subsided hours later when he was told that Danny Abrahamson was out sick with a viral infection and wouldn't be back for at least a month.

After work, Cosmo left a message on Phyllis's phone.

'Will take you up on your dare. See you in the bar, tomorrow night.'

Now all Cosmo had to worry about was what to write? He wanted to elevate the standard. No 'I want to stick my spunk filled stick of dynamite up your orifice of joy' for Cosmo Kincaid! He was looking for something more worthy. Even profound. Later that night, he found just the thing. He was tidying up his spare room and located an old diary he'd written during his last year in Business College. On April 19th 1985, the entry read: Professor Egan was lecturing about diminishing marginal returns today when Timothy King turned to me and said something interesting, 'Life is a series of diminishing marginal surprises.'

Phyllis smiled as she placed the drinks on the table.

'Can't believe you took me up on the dare. What's the line again?'

'Life is a series of diminishing marginal surprises. Says it all really.'

Cosmo touched the Primo Jet Super black marker pen in his inner jacket pocket. He watched various men get up, go and return from the Gents. The random nature of visits to the Gents in public houses always fascinated him. Sometimes when a bar is packed, the Gents can remain empty for fifteen minutes. Other times when it is less packed there can be a huge turnover in urination proceedings.

He stood up abruptly.

'Now is the time, Phyllis. I will see you presently.'

'Good luck.'

Cosmo opened the door of the Gents. Both cubicles were engaged. He stood waiting. Various men entered and used the urinals beside him, some texting while urinating – Darwinian evolution continues apace – finally, a cubicle became free. Ignoring the farmyard stench, Cosmo entered briskly and pulled at his Primo Jet Super black marker pen. He found a blank space on the toilet wall. He cowered. He felt an endorphin-driven giddiness as he started to write clearly in block capitals. Life is... suddenly, the sound of flushing in the cubicle next door. Cosmo turned round. He then heard a cough and looked up. The extremely tall man – older with timc but still very much alive – looked down on him. Startled, Cosmo fumbled the black marker pen and dropped it down the toilet. The extremely tall man stooped over the partition, and peered, trying to decipher what Cosmo had written.

'Life is a series of dim...'

He paused for a moment.

'I like it.'

THE LIFE AND DEATH OF AN OBSCURE IRISH ACTOR

Born in Dublin, one hundred years ago today, Bertram Joyce – Ireland's answer to Donald Sinden – was from an early age obsessed with *Hamlet*. Planning a career in the legal profession, his life changed forever at the age of nineteen, when his father was found mysteriously murdered in the back garden of their home in Denmark Street and his mother Gertie set up home with his Uncle Claude.

Unable to confront his uncle about the suspicious circumstances of his father's death and the subsequent domestic arrangement with his mother, Bertram rashly decided to become an actor and cooked up a bizarre plan. He vowed to spend all his inheritance money putting on productions of *Hamlet* in towns and villages all over Ireland and performing the lead role himself. Inviting his mother and uncle to the performances, he would, whilst on stage or standing in the wings, constantly gauge their reaction. They invariably walked out just after 'the play within the play' scene, not because they were feeling guilt-ridden and uncomfortable but because the productions were usually so appallingly bad. As the famed theatre critic Aubrey Davenport noted pithily after one woeful show in Portlaoise, 'To be elsewhere, or not to be elsewhere – that is the question!'

Reacting badly to persistent dismal reviews and feeling his ingenious strategy to expose his uncle was proving unsuccessful, Bertram decided to cut all ties with his family in 1935 and move to London to perfect his craft. For a young thespian to acquire the necessary skills and experience in those days, it was best to join a repertory company. Bertram did just that, coming under the wing of the legendary and flamboyant actor-manager Montague Keeble.

Renowned for conducting rehearsals in his silk pyjamas, Montague instilled in the young actor a complete lack of technique and an over-reliance on rouge. And by mid-1936, Montague gave the young Irish tragedian a qualified vote of confidence by making him his dresser's dresser. Each evening before the performance, Bertram had to painstakingly dress Montague's dresser, Bunty de Marney, before Bunty went to work to dress Montague. After six months of this tedium, Bertram confronted Montague and told him he wanted to act! Impressed by the young Irishman's gumption, Montague promoted Bertram a step closer to the stage. He was made the understudy's understudy.

Bertram waited patiently for his English debut. And waited. And waited. One night during a production of *King Lear*, Montague, playing the lead, came down with appendicitis, and his understudy, a very young Peter Finch replaced him. When Peter Finch broke his arm, with Montague still convalescing in hospital, Bertram at last sensed his chance, but at that very moment he was called home to Ireland for his mother's funeral. She had inexplicably drunk from a cup of wine with poison pellets in it.

He returned to England in a restless and depressed state. With health fully restored to Montague and Peter Finch, Bertram became increasingly worried that he would never get the chance to act – within his own lifetime – if he remained in Montague's troupe.

He sought employment elsewhere and eventually became a jobbing actor. After many years doing the rounds, playing in small theatres and staying in damp boarding houses, he became quite established in theatrical circles as 'Bertram Joyce – The Actor with the Bellowing Voice'.

Sir Anthony Quayle, who was just starting off on a successful career, recalled years later, 'Bertram, the darling boy, was such a bad actor that anytime he'd make an entrance, the audience would either fall asleep and snore or chat amongst themselves. I think he was playing Malvolio during a matinee in Torquay opposite a radiant Peggy Ashcroft, when he made his entrance and everybody just picked up their newspapers and started to read. To attract the audience's attention he started shouting his lines. And that's when Bertram Joyce – The Actor with the Bellowing Voice was born.'

When Bertram was in his full braying form, he began sounding remarkably like Winston Churchill. And throughout the Second World War, he was part of a group of actors that staged shows in the London Underground during air raids. For those members of the public who stayed for the shows, his bombastic staccato delivery caused much comment and unintentional laughter. Others would already be on their journey home, happier to leave the performance and face the uncertainty of the blitz.

However, British Intelligence decided to utilize him to impersonate Churchill for radio broadcasts, as a decoy to fool the Germans. 'Operation Ham' proved remarkably successful. After the war, the Rank Organization wanted to make a movie on the subject. Bertram was asked to read for the main role and play himself. Sadly he failed the audition. To add insult to injury, Peter Finch got the role.

By the early 1950s, Bertram's style of camp histrionics and unbearable overacting seemed quite dated. He found it difficult to find the right parts and drifted into long periods of 'resting'. To alleviate his boredom he started to write. He had become a big fan of some American writers including Tennessee Williams, and in the summer of 1952, attempted to write a play, which in retrospect was heavily derivative of *A Streetcar Named Desire*. Once completed, the manuscript of *A Tram Called Lust* was sent to renegade theatre director Nigel MacBeth. Nigel loved the play and insisted on directing it and putting Bertram in the leading role. It was the beginning of a long and pointless collaboration.

Every production Nigel MacBeth was ever involved in ended in disaster. Suspicious theatrical folk maintain this is because his name was 'MacBeth', and as he demanded to be called 'Mr MacBeth' during rehearsals, this broke the timeworn theatrical taboo about uttering that particular word in a theatre. Others meanwhile claim it was because Nigel was a completely talentless oaf. Whatever the reason, the production of 'Tram', as it became known, was the absolute nadir of Bertram's career. His attempts at a Louisiana accent were much derided.

Aubrey Davenport, the venerable theatre critic who had slated Bertram during his formative years in Ireland and who subsequently ended up working for *The London Times,* wrote in his review, 'Why does this man act? He doesn't have presence – he has absence.'

Bertram Joyce returned to Ireland in the late 1970s. He moved back into his family home where his elderly Uncle Claude resided. Still incapable of bringing up the family's past with his uncle, he took to renting out videocassettes of the various film and TV versions of *Hamlet* over the years and screening them nightly. This caused much tension between them and was attributed as the cause of the knife fight in their living-room that led to both their deaths in 1983.

THE DON OF THE DANCE

Hollywood has come to Borris-on-Ossary. And it's all because of mammy.

Might as well start at the beginning, 'twas the strangest occurrence that happened for donkey's years. Sometime in June 1997, Joey Provolone drove into town. There I was minding my own business in the shop when these two fellas in sharp suits walk in.

'The boss wants to talk to you.'

They escorted me to this big black sedan and opened the car door. I got in the back.

'My name is Joey Provolone. Entrepreneur.'

'Pascal Geraghty. Shopkeeper.'

He took off his sunglasses.

'Is your mother Bridie Geraghty?'

'Yes.'

'I want to meet her.'

'Why?'

He handed me a folded newspaper article. I read the headline. 'Dance Superstar Michael Flatley praises former teacher.' Joey cupped his hands.

'You know that thing, epiphany, that moment when you suddenly see things differently. Well, I saw *Riverdance* last year on Broadway. I didn't even want to go, Gina dragged me along... but when I saw Michael Flatley dancing, I don't know, I felt so alive... I thought to myself, I want to learn how to friggin' do that.'

I looked at Joey. Could be tricky. Not only did he carry a bit of weight, as they say, but he seemed to have an unnaturally large crotch. Marrow-sized. A physical abnormality not wholly compatible with vigorous hopping and leaping.

He leaned towards me.

'You know what they call me back in Hoboken? Joey Five Testicles. I got a bigger set of cojones than anyone in this... uh...'

Sidekick number one intervened. 'Solar system, boss.'

'Right, and if I set my mind to do something, I do it. *Capisce*? '

I nodded.

'Now, I want your mother, Bridie Geraghty, of Borris-on-Ossary, County Laois, Ireland,' he pointed at the newspaper article, 'the greatest Irish dancing teacher of them all, according to Mr Flatley, to help me dance like Mr Flatley.'

Think fast Pascal, I thought. Don't want to be dragging mammy in with this bunch.

'She hasn't given a class for years. She's not well. She's dead. Well, not dead, but not great.'

Clarity, Pascal. Clarity.

'She's had a stroke, a massive stroke, divil the movement out of her, and her so sprightly and all in her heyday. She'll be teaching no more jigs and reels, I'll tell you that much.'

Joey sighed.

Then sidekick number two piped up.

'Let's see if his story pans out, boss. We'll go visit the dame.'

Over the decades, I wondered about the point of going to mass every week. Like, will I ever benefit in the long run? Or am just wasting my time? While sitting in the back of the big black sedan, I realized here was my pay-off. An old neighbour was in a quasi-comatose state in the nearest nursing home. And – thank you God, sorry for ever *ever* doubting you – her name was also Bridie. Bridie Prendergast.

We parked in the driveway of St Conleth's Community Care Centre. Joey struggled to get out of the car and waddled towards the front steps. And he wants to dance like Flatley! Delusions are a thing to behold. But I didn't have the time to ponder such profound human truths. I had to enter the building first, mumble introductions and try to find Bridie Prendergast.

'Can I help you gentlemen?'

The nurse at reception hid her slight surprise at my three companions who were standing a few feet behind me. I leaned forward and whispered.

'Some of Bridie Prendergast's family. From America. Have come over to see her.'

'Room fifty-six, down the corridor to the left. She's very popular today. In fact, your mother is with her at the moment.'

Sometimes you hear sentences uttered to you in life that stop you dead in your tracks. This was like one of those sentences but with a locomotive running over you at the same time.

Thoughts flooded my cranium. Not necessarily in this order. County Laois is a small place. The nurse knew who I was all along. I never knew mammy was a friend of Bridie Prendergast. It most definitely was a complete waste of time going to mass all these years. What will I do now? And oh yeh, I am a dead man.

Think fast, Pascal. Again.

I turned to Joey.

'They are changing her sheets. We'll have to wait a bit. Maybe we'll go outside and sit in the car.'

'How long does it take to change sheets? We can sit here.'

We sat in the waiting area. My eyes were fixed on the corridor. I had an idea.

'Listen, I'll go in and see if they are finished.'

I hurried to room fifty-six. Bridie Prendergast was sitting up in bed. Pleasantly impassive. No sign of mammy. I ran out. Mammy had just come out of the ladies. And was passing the waiting area. She noticed Joey. She smiled at him. He smiled back. She was walking out the door. Everything was going to be fine. Then the nurse at reception said 'Bridie, did you catch your son Pascal inside?'

The strange thing is, Joey was very reasonable about the misunderstandings, the mix-ups – alright – the lies. He stayed about a week in Borris and mammy gave him a few lessons.

'Better than you'd think' was her verdict.

Joey went back to the States, and over the years I sometimes wondered whatever happened him. That was until this morning when I picked up *The Laois Nationalist* and read a story about a film being made nearby called *The Don of The Dance* about an Irish-dancing champion Mafioso who learned all he knew from a local dance teacher. A padded Christopher Walken plays Joey, the ever-radiant Helen Mirren plays mammy but why they had to go pick John C. Reilly to play yours truly I'll never know. But, I suppose that's Hollywood for you!

ANOTHER MEETING WITH SISYPHUS

'Karl.'

'Sisyphus. Thanks for seeing me.'

'Take a seat. Hang on – just have to finish this call – so what's the builders' name, love? Oh. And did you look up their website? Yeh? What? It said 'currently under construction'? Arey, listen Fidelma darling, we'll look into it later, I have someone here with me in the office, bye love, bye, bye.'

'Getting some work done in the house?'

'Yeh. Extending the living-room out the back a bit. That's the plan, anyway. So how are things with you?'

'Ok.'

'By the way, have you ever heard of Cassie Foy?'

'Yeh. They say her work is like 'Maeve Binchy on Benzedrine'.'

'Yeh? She's looking for representation. What's she like?'

'Dunno. Probably the New Next Big Already Forgotten Thing. Haven't read any of her stuff. I don't read other writers.'

'Oh. Yeh. Listen talking about that eh, the first thing I have to say, I never got round to reading those first few stories you left with me. Sorry about that. I've been up to my ears with this auld extension to the house and other matters.'

'Oh. I see. I brought three others with me.'

'Oh, leave them with me. Alright? Look, I'm setting aside a few hours on Saturday. Promise. Now Karl, did you have any thoughts on those other ideas we talked about the last day?'

'Not really. I haven't developed a drink problem in the interim. I don't think I've got testicular cancer since, uh... a man did try to sell me some drugs in the gents of a well-known hostelry but...'

'The auld mindfulness thing?'

'No.'

'Well, maybe you have a think about it. And do you know what else sells loads, Karl?'

'What?'

'Books about the Holocaust. They always lap them up.'

'I know. I visited Dachau last year, by the way. With Rachel. Spooky place. And everybody around us kept taking selfies. Not just teenagers. But their parents! I thought, do they not understand the word inappropriate? What sort of world are we living in?'

'Jesus! *Selfies at Dachau*. What a title. It just grabs you! And reels you in! I can see it already. They'd love discussing a title like that on *The Book Programme*. Now, listen, I'm just talking off the top of my head, but, but, but, let me finish, don't make that face, but, how about working on a slim volume, about, uh, you know like a rumination, like, on historical events receding, like, and uh, a discursive meditation on memory and the lost voices of the past and all that sort of carry on. There'd be a huge market for it!'

'Discursive meditation?! Sisyphus, are you *on* something? No. No. No. No. I think that whole tragic topic and era has been amply covered over the years.'

'Arey, I'm only trying to help out. You know what else they love this weather, books about the funny things Irish people say and do. Books with lists in them.'

'Yeh. I tried working on one of those a few years back. *The Emerald Almanac*.'

'Really? Was it any good?'

'I lost interest. Ended up being just pages of listicles.'

'What?'

'Listicles. An article or book with nothing but lists. The scourge of the internet age. A celebration of humanity's new-found limited attention span. They're everywhere. *List*icular cancer.'

'Well, say what you like but they're very popular. Maybe take that old idea out of the drawer, have a look at it again. I've come up with one or two myself. One of the chapters could be like uh... list of things Irish people do in restaurants, like they never complain like, everything alright with your meal? Yeh, it was lovely but it was really shite like, you know what I mean! And uh... and uh, let me see... uh... other things like that.'

'Well, that's a product of our post-colonial hangover, of course. Irish people are afraid to complain because of our colonial legacy. If we complained in the old days we'd be put in jail or even put up against a wall and shot.'

'Right but no historical insights and stuff, save that for *Selfies at Dachau*, just funny headings and lists and things. Fidelma says publishers love those sort of books, ideal for presents, bit of a laugh, people put them in their loos like and you can pick them up while you are doing your business.'

'Laughing while defecating? Not sure if that juxtaposition of activities is advisable or even possible.'

'Look, you can come up with all the quips you want but all Sisyphus O'Shea is doing is trying to help. The internet has re-written the rule book about the book, like, and uh, you have to adapt with the times. Publishing has gone to the dogs. You sink. Or you swim. And these types of books swim. Now Fidelma came up with a title, *Mad Feckers – The Mad Feckin' Things Irish People Say and Do*. What do you think?'

'I preferred *Me and My Mindfulness*.'

'Look, Karl, the trouble with you is you are too negative! The Abominable No-man. No. No. No. No. All I'm trying to do is to keep SOS Management going and trying to keep everyone happy, alright? Now, I'll read the auld stories at the weekend, I'm man of my word, but we'll all have to think of other possible projects. The landscape in publishing is changing, the Teutonic plates are shifting.'

'Tectonic.'

'Tectonic. Teutonic. Doesn't matter. It's only words. And people are reading less and less words all the time. Alright? And that's why the auld Mad Feckers idea could be the way to go. So, listen, I'll be in touch and we'll have a chat about those stories of yours, but we'll have to have a few more balls up in the air, alright? Right, I'll see you then Karl, and remember, keep the flag flying!'

THE THREE EXTRA STORIES LEFT WITH SISYPHUS

GODFREY GIVE ME

Addiction is a terrible thing. I knew all about it when I was eight. That was when I developed my bizarre and unhealthy communion wafer dependency.

I had my first communion on the day of my First Communion. Figures. Maybe it was the connection between being dressed up in an expensive new outfit and lavished with all that attention but when I tasted, for the very first time, that wafer thin wheat flour and water I was hooked. I wanted it again. And again. And again.

I decided to become a daily communicant. The following evening, I went to mass after school. At the appropriate time, I approached the altar and knelt down for my fix. I was given just the one. Was that all? Fr Tobin continued down the altar railing. Giving each parishioner just the one. Just the one! I needed more. Much more.

I did some research on Christian Doctrine. Ok, I asked my dad. He knew all about these things.

'Dad, how many communions are you allowed have a day?'

'One.'

'Is that all?'

'Two if you happen to go to a wedding and a funeral on the same day, but how often does that happen?'

I made some calculations. My auntie Brenda was very ill and my older cousin Jarleth was engaged, but yes what were the chances.

'Three, in the extreme case, when it is requested by someone who is in danger of and is almost guaranteed imminent death.'

Faking a near death illness, though not impossible, seemed a very tricky proposition to pull off, and for all that work, just the three communion wafers?

'What happens, if you have more than three?'

Dad smiled.

'You get to work on that lobster-red suntan with Lucifer. For eternity.'

Getting subterranean sunburn didn't scare me. After that stealthy sun attack in Lahinch the previous summer where my skin had slowly barbecued, my freckle count had increased threefold and my childhood nickname 'small fry' had finally begun to make sense, I felt I could survive anything. Anyway, my craving for those tiny white circular delicacies overrode all concern, fear and guilt. I had to get to the source. The next day I signed up to become an altar boy.

It took three weeks of serving mass before I had the chance to hit the jackpot. Three weeks of ringing the bell. Shaking the thurible. Moving pew cushions. The endless bowing, genuflecting, kneeling. Can you imagine the orthopedic damage to a young boy's long term posture? And what, pray tell, (apt use of expression given the surroundings) was the purpose of the paten? That golden table tennis racket-like implement held under a parishioner's chin on delivery, from priest's hand to parishioner's mouth, of communion wafer. Communion wafer doesn't drip! But I set aside all these grumbles. I had one aim. To get at the stuff in the golden safety box in the corner. My tabernacle of kaleidoscopic dreams.

I bided my time. Finally, I got my opportunity. It was an early morning mass. Smallish congregation. Sleep-deprived priest. Afterwards, having changed out of my surplices and soutanes, I noticed Fr Tobin had left the key in the tabernacle door. Now was my chance. I looked around. Sneaked onto the altar. Trembling. Anticipation-fueled. I slowly turned the key. I peered in. Silver chalices. Cruets. Then, at the back. Sparkly and white. I saw them. All lined up there. My happy hosts. My wacky wafers. My jazz eucharists. I could contain myself no longer. I grabbed at them. I gobbled down a mouthful. The hit was sensational. Suddenly I heard footsteps. I stuffed as many as I could in the already bulky pockets – chewing gum, tissue, marbles, football cards – of my short pants and made my escape.

That afternoon, up a tree near the house, I gorged myself. All those communion wafers. Must have been some record. But by early evening the post-euphoric down was kicking in. As was the guilt. If over three in the one day sent you to hell, where does twenty-eight land you? Pondering this, I was particularly quiet at mealtime.

'Are you not going to finish your fish fingers, love?'

'Mammy, I'm not really that hungry.'

Trouble was by the next day, I'd forgotten the guilt and needed my dose again. New codes of practice had been implemented overnight concerning tabernacle security. If only I'd thought about replicating the key. Damn you! Fuzzy-thinking sacramental bread junkie! So where would I get my gear from now on? And the right amount for my needs? There was only one person I could turn to. Godfrey Curley.

Fort Baxter had Ernie Bilko. Peckham had 'Del Boy' Trotter. We had Godfrey Curley. Anything. Anytime. Anywhere. For a price. I sought him out in the school shed at break-time. I told him what I needed. He told me, no problem. He had an inside contact with the Sisters of Poor Clare who produced the stuff. He mentioned a price. A pocket money increase would never cover it. All the same I agreed.

I met him the following Monday. In a car park behind the newly opened shopping centre. Why did we meet in a car park? I guess we were watching too many American cop shows on TV. We looked quite conspicuous straddling insecurely on our slightly oversized bikes. The neighbours' wives were all coming and going in their new Datsuns, Mirafioris and Opel Kadetts, waving at me and wondering how my Auntie Brenda was. I couldn't take the tension. Maybe I wasn't made for this sordid life of crime. When the coast was finally clear, Godfrey handed me over a sample of the batch. I tasted it. It was pure. Really good quality. These nuns knew what they were doing.

'Do you want the rest?'

'Yeh.'

'Money first.'

I took the small knapsack from my back, and removed a red piggy-bank.

'This wasn't part of the deal. A swift exchange is what we agreed on!'

I counted out the money in pennies, shillings and pounds. I handed him the exact amount. He pocketed the coins quickly. Suddenly I had a strange feeling. I looked up at the sky.

'God forgive me.'

But then I looked at the bag of goodies.

'Now Godfrey. Give me.'

CUPID BICUSPID

My psychologist told me to smile more.

'It's scientifically proven. It will make you feel better. Your brain will release endorphins.'

She grinned. It scared me a little.

'Even if you have to pretend. Just try it. When walking down the street for example.'

I never liked to smile. But she was my psychologist.

'Ok.'

I left her office. Moved my facial muscles gradually from a grimace to a smile. And for a moment, a fleeting moment, I think, maybe, I did start to feel happy. Then some passing pedestrian caught my eye. He didn't like what he saw. Turned around and punched me. Hard. In the mouth. Dislodging a bicuspid. Which had a crown. That needed replacing. Which caused a weakness in the tooth next to it. That needed to be extracted. Leading to extensive bridge-work and further re-alignment in the upper left quadrant. Total cost €2,400. All because Dr Kathleen Harrold told me to smile more.

I felt that this was not fair. I decided to do something about it. Like retrieve the money. Somehow. And forget lawyers! Go the direct route was my thinking. I was honest, though. Only wanted back what was owed me. Not a cent more, not a cent less. It was the principle. I decided to enlist the help of my friend, Ross. More trifling criminal than petty criminal. But competent for the proposed job at hand. A plan was devised. Sunglasses and some slightly ill-fitting headgear were acquired.

Every week, Dr Harrold's secretary, Kim, transferred the earnings from Dr Harrold's practice to a bank in Rathgar. All we had to do was intercept Kim. After she had her usual coffee in the local coffee shop.

We observed her from a corner table. I looked at Ross. He looked at Kim. He seemed lost in thought.

'Are you alright?'

No response.

'Ross. No one's going to be hurt. We just bump into her, grab the bag, run, go somewhere safe, I count out the €2,400 – not a cent more, not a cent less – return the surplus and never listen to a psychologist again!'

He sighed. Shook his head.

'You know in all those movies, in all those books, or in biographies, and the guy is sitting down, and he looks across a crowded room and sees a woman and he announces to all and sundry, that's the woman I'm going to marry and spend the rest of my life with... well, and I know this is probably not the appropriate time, but that's the woman I'm going to spend the rest of my life with!'

I was dumbfounded.

There was a long pause.

'Can we rob her first?'

Ross stared at me. I argued the point. Weakly.

'My €2,400. It's the principle. Not a cent more, not a cent less.'

He removed his shades.

'If you lay a finger on that woman – my future wife, the mother of my unborn children, the woman I shall grow old with – I will maim you.'

He stood up. Took off his ushanka. Walked purposefully over to Kim. I crouched down hoping she wouldn't see me. He tentatively started to talk to her. At first she reacted shyly, but she warmed to him and seemed quite smitten as he pulled up a chair and sat next her. Cupid was working overtime. Not just one arrow. A quiver full.

Two months later they got engaged. A marriage date was set. Ross asked me to be his best man. I immediately regretted saying yes.

Not only was I, now, €2,400 out of pocket, but I had to make a speech in front of a group of strangers.

If there was one thing I disliked more than smiling it was speaking in public. I needed advice. What should I do? Also, what could I put in the speech? Ross had supplied me with some vague biographical details, but having edited all mentions of his slightly felonious past, some of it comical, I had very little to work with.

'Ross, please let me mention that time you hijacked a passing car after robbing a post office, but the police had no problem picking you up because you were stuck in the middle of that funeral cortege.'

'No, because (a) I look stupid and (b) I'm a changed man.'

'But what do I say in the speech?'

'I don't know. Look up the internet. Buy a joke book.'

I spent weeks agonizing over a hodge-podge of hoary old best man jokes and banal patter. The big day was approaching. My anxiety levels were rocketing. I was mainlining on Xanax and chamomile tea. One morning I even knocked back a whole dropper bottle of Bach's Rescue Remedy. How would I get through that speech? I was left with no choice. I needed help.

Dr Harrold sat back on her specially designed orthopedically tested psychologists' chair. She thought about my predicament.

'Imagine the wedding guests naked.'

'But being Kim's boss, you'll be there Dr Harrold. I'll be imagining you naked. Should I be imaging my psychologist naked?'

'Try to relax. Listen to your breathing.'

'There'll be no breathing. I'll be dead. Having to make that speech will kill me.'

'Just try it. Breathe in. Breathe out. '

I tried it. Futile.

'How can I listen to my breathing when I'm in the middle of trying to remember my lines? That sounds like multi-tasking to me. Not a strong point for most men.'

She paused.

'Smile. It will make you feel better and it will help the wedding guests relax.'

I tried smiling. She continued.

'You really should smile more. Releases endorphins. Scientifically proven.'

She then peered over her glasses and scrutinized me.

'By the way, did you get some dental work done?'

URSULA'S BOOK PROBLEM

I had this problem. Over the last eighteen months, I kept getting books as presents from a friend. However, that friend had different tastes in books than me. So I wanted to give these books away. To my local charity shop. The trouble is, my friend shopped in the local charity shop. He didn't give presents of the books he bought in the local charity shop – he was not a cheapskate – but he did shop there, so I couldn't leave the books he gave me in that charity shop. You see, he always inscribed his presents. Now, the nearest charity shop outside of town was forty miles away. And since I couldn't afford to replace my car after being rear-ended by that Hiace van last year, my limited living space was filling up with unread books. I asked my friend Catriona if she could drive to the other charity shop with the books – must have been twenty books at this stage, he gave me lots of presents, I guess he liked me – but she made a very good point that he could be out of town sometime and pop into that other charity shop and then he would see all the books he had given me over the past two years and it would devastate him, seeing them all lined up in that shop. I couldn't do that to him.

They were mainly crime books. He loved crime. I wasn't that pushed about crime books. It was always the same thing. Down-at-heel loner private eye with a drink problem. Dysfunctional relationship with a drug addict daughter. Solving ever-improbable clues leading to an ever-predictable climax. Catriona told me I should just tell him I didn't like crime books. But I couldn't. It would be like insulting him or something. So then I came up with this plan. Ask Catriona to maybe spread out the delivery of books over five or six charity shops around the whole county of Galway. She agreed. I made the sandwiches and stumped up for the petrol.

His name was Tom. Gangly and well-mannered. A widower. He used to be in show business. Did a novelty country music act in the late 1970s in the States. Called himself Beauregard Kierkegaard, the philosophising redneck. He was no redneck. Not much of a philosopher either. Although he once turned to me and glumly stated that the uterus of America is the barrel of a gun. I did think about that one for days.

We first met in a coffee shop. That morning, Catriona was meant to pick me up to go to the chiropractor's but was late and the battery on my mobile phone was low, so I asked the man sitting across from me, if I could use his mobile phone to ring her. And pay him whatever was owed of course. He said no problem. So I rang Catriona with his phone. Catriona didn't answer so I left a message on her mobile. I returned his phone.

We started to chat. Five minutes later his phone rang. He answered. It was a confused Catriona. He handed me his phone. I was ever so embarrassed and flustered. Catriona was all curious. She told me whoever it was had a lovely voice. I told him. 'My friend says you have a lovely voice.' 'I'm Tom, by the way.' 'I'm Ursula.'

You know those May to December romances. Tom and I were more like an October to December romance. Without the romance. We were more like friends. I hadn't been with anybody since Jasper died over five years ago. And frankly, I didn't miss it. Most men are silent maniacs. Jasper was. Couldn't make up my mind yet about Tom.

Then the most dreadful thing happened. Tom popped around unexpectedly the following Sunday. The day after Catriona and I had spent the whole of Saturday, driving over 120 miles to eight charity shops in the Greater Galway region and even taking in south Mayo and north Clare. To dispose of Tom's presents. Of course, I invited him in. He'd never been to my place before. I'd been to his place once or twice. For no hanky panky, mind you. He fixed me a risotto once. Which was not a culinary success. He'd used the wrong sort of rice. And stock. And everything. Anyway, I was just out of the shower and needed to go dry my hair so I told him to sit and wait. When I returned, he was looking at my bookshelf. I live in a small modestly-sized apartment – sold up the house nearly three years ago – but I cherish my books. Obviously not Tom's. He was too polite to say anything but I could see he was a little deflated. I felt awful. I gave him a cup of tea and we had a sort of strained chat. I should have held on to the books until he'd moved away, became infirm or died or something. I didn't know if we'd be friends any more. I would miss him in his own way. I'd also miss the presents. Who else gave me presents? Here was this man giving me presents and I wanted to give them away. How could I have been so cruel?

Catriona was not best pleased when I suggested a return trip to the eight charity shops. I insisted that I needed to retrieve those books. Invite Tom over for dinner and have them prominently displayed on my bookshelf. After a second day-long 120 mile round trip we recovered sixteen. Obviously Ed Wycherley's *Tough Guy Shenanigans* trilogy found a new home in Ballinasloe and Val Thursby's interminable *The Dead Don't Smile* was gone from that little shop in Clifden.

Catriona came up with an idea. Tell him the books he gave me are very popular with my friends. The last time he visited they had all been lent out. But now most of them have been returned.

On Wednesday evening Tom arrived for dinner. I fixed him some risotto. Proper rice. Proper stock. A nice bottle of white wine. A very pleasant soirée. I felt attracted to him for the first time. In *that* way. He'd even bought me another book. Asimov. He smiled at me.

'I love science fiction. Do you?'

I thought of the future. Not in the daily trips to Neptune science fiction sense. But in my cramped apartment sense. Book shelves being laden down with unopened galaxy–centric tomes. I looked over at Tom.

'Yes. Even more than crime books.'

A CUP OF COFFEE WITH OLD FRIEND ALAN

'I hate people who mix up Ryan Reynolds and Ryan Gosling.'

'Alan, it's the times we live in. No one knows anything anymore. So much mixing up nowadays. There's Lotte Lenya and Lene Lovich. That always leads to confusion.'

'That's understandable, Karl. Both reasonably obscure footnotes at this stage.'

'I disagree. Lotte Lenya, a major cultural figure in 1920s Germany. Lene Lovich, a mere one-hit wonder.'

'Point accepted. What about Romy Schneider and Roy Scheider?'

'For starters, lazy. Woman. Man. Austrian. American. '

'Van Heflin and Van Halen?'

'Insane. One is a craggy-faced Hollywood actor from the 1950s, the other an over-rated embarrassing rock outfit from the 1980s!'

'Van Helsing and Van Halen?'

'I don't think anyone would confuse Van Helsing with Van Halen.'

'Ok. Sandy Dennis and Sandy Denny?'

'More nuanced than the whole Schneider and Scheider muddle. The names are very similar, the sex is the same and they were both in the public eye during the same era. The clueless perpetrator should be punished but one can see where the puzzlement would arise.'

'Admirable point.'

'And most importantly, Alan, they both died tragically young. One fell out a window, one fell down the stairs, so a suspended sentence is in order in this case. I would put these two in the same category as Steely Dan and Steeleye Span.'

'I concur.'

'L.P. Hartley's *The Go-Between* and The Go-Between's first LP?'

'Ha-ha. How about Fats Waller and Fats Domino?'

'That's another Gosling and Reynolds aberration. Unforgiveable!'

'One I hate, Karl, is *Donnie Darko* and *Donnie Brasco*! How anyone can mix up one of the greatest movies, ever, about teenage alienation, nightmares and giant rabbits and an over-rated wise guy movie, I'll never understand.'

'Alan, *Donnie Darko* is unadulterated impenetrable hogwash.'

'I beg to differ.'

'Let's drop it. Where were we? Yes, here's another one. This is the worst one I've ever heard! Muhammad Ali versus George Formby in the Rumble in the Jungle in 1974. That is just downright bonkers.'

'But hilarious! We come up with such funny stuff

when we just riff off each other. We should do a podcast or something.'

'What?'

'We should try podcasting, Karl.'

'Podcasting? That's just people talking about stuff.'

'I know. Like what we're just doing! Everyone is doing it. Helps with your profile.'

'But Alan, it's just guys talking or women talking. It's just talking. People talking about things! I can get that on the radio. I can get that on the TV and with added pictures too.'

'Yeh. But fewer people listen to the radio and watch TV. Everything is consumed online. Podcasting. Increases your brand awareness. People can listen to it on their smartphones. Huge outreach. I mean, *you* should do it at least, you being in the creative area.'

'Brand awareness! Outreach! It's just more background noise, Alan. It's just something else for people to do and tweet about madly, while instagramming their avocado toast, as they make another desperate plea for notice in a cyber-swamp of ego and neediness.'

'Just trying to give you some ideas. Could have me on as a guest. And that's another thing, talking of Twitter. You really should set up a Twitter account.'

'I have one. Set one up last year. I have 6k followers.'

'What?!'

'Without the k.'

'Oh. Well, listen we can follow each other. What

about a blog? You're a writer.'

'Tried it for a while about four years ago. Called it *A Moan Again, Naturally*.'

'Anyone check it out? Any feedback? Ok, don't worry. Blogs are *so* noughties at this stage. But think about the podcasting. It is all the rage, at the moment. People in all lines of work are doing it.'

'Who'd listen to me, Alan? Who would I talk to?'

'Apart from me? I don't know. Other writers.'

'Why? It would just be a bunch of depressed people using the term 're-imagining' a lot and self-consciously sniggering at their outré literary references.'

'Just an idea, Karl.'

'By the way, uh... did you ever get round to reading my stories?'

'Eh, about the stories...'

'Don't say, you didn't read those three stories I sent you. For fuck sake.'

'I'm sorry. I had them set aside last Thursday night, but then Aoife wanted to go out to get something to eat. So we go into Ranelagh to go to our favourite restaurant, but when we got there and were all set to sit down, Aoife saw someone sitting at a near-by table she knew, but she couldn't remember the person's name. So to avoid an embarrassing situation, where Aoife would have to introduce me to this person whose name she couldn't remember, she decided that we should leave the restaurant and walk around the area for half an hour. We spent much of that time going through a list of female names alphabetically while getting very wet. After forty-five minutes, having got to 'Pauline – no', we return to the restaurant. I'm getting very hungry and irritable at this stage but Aoife insists, since question mark is still there...'

'Question mark?'

'The woman that Aoife knew, because question mark is still there we have to find somewhere else to eat. I curse question mark. She must be one of the slowest eaters in the Dublin 6 area. How long does it take to eat a plate of vegetarian noodles? So I'm very agitated and of course feeling guilty about not reading your stories, I'm thinking, I should read the stories my friend wrote, I've had them for nearly six weeks now, anyway, myself and Aoife walk around some more in post-torrential pre-apocalyptic rain and we eventually end up having a disintegrating falafel – more fell than fala – and some garlic pummeled baba ganoush in The Gaza Strip Joint in Dunville Avenue. Have you ever been there?'

'The Gaza Strip Joint?'

'Yeh. They do great spinach filo rolls.'

'No.'

'I swear, I'll get round to reading those stories.'

'Alan, it's fine. Did you ever find out her name?'

'Who?'

'The woman. Question mark.'

'Oh. By the time we got home, Aoife had narrowed it down. It was either Theodora or Dorothea.'

'I hate people who mix up Theodora and Dorothea.'
'Ha! Nice one. Listen, I'll get you another coffee.'

THE STORIES ALAN HAS YET TO READ

A CHRISTMAS BELL

I was ten. And well aware I should be existing in a post-fluffy toy world. But I had fallen in love with that sky blue fluffy rabbit in Glynn's Toy Shop. And Christmas was coming up.

Mother was understanding. Father was traumatized.

There was another complication – apart from Father being traumatized. The fluffy rabbit had an internal bell. And anytime you picked up the fluffy rabbit the bell rang. I didn't like that. The bell reminded me that at my age I shouldn't be fraternizing with this fluffy rabbit. That I should be acutely ashamed and embarrassed. That I should be requesting Scalextric or Subbuteo for Christmas.

Or Action Man.

That bell had to be excised.

'No problem', mother said. 'I can remove the bell from the bunny.'

'Could you stop describing it as a bunny? Just call it a rabbit.' I said.

Mother nodded and continued.

'I can open it up, remove the bell, sew it back up again with my needle and thread. Problem solved.'

I thought that's all very well, Mother, but you are forgetting about your – legendary in family circles – inept sewing skills. I can't let you go near that rabbit. Thanks, anyway.

Father's sister, my auntie Cora, was a dab hand at embroidery and in former times a champion seamstress. She had to be approached.

But there was a dilemma. Father did not want to publicize the fact, in front of his family, that his son, who would turn eleven in February, wanted a fluffy toy for Christmas.

I made a suggestion. 'Dad, just tell Auntie Cora the fluffy rabbit is for Anne Marie.'

Anne Marie was my kid sister. Seven-years-old. One problem. She was extremely precocious. She was the one who told *me* there was no Santa Claus. Also, she happened to be in the room when I made the suggestion.

'No way, Dad. I wouldn't be caught dead near that fluffy rabbit,' she announced while putting down her recent birthday present, a hardback edition of *Crime and Punishment*.'I don't want you telling anybody I'd like a toy like that for Christmas! I would find that kind of behavior highly patronizing and incredibly offensive!'

It was already December 19th. Children were in bed. Parents were eating some leftovers.

'First things first,' Mother declared to Father while scooping out some re-heated Moussaka from the cooking tray – she'd been to Thessaloniki the previous autumn with the local Arts and Crafts Committee – 'We have to make sure we get that bunny rabbit. There is only the one left and we can sort out the bell later.'

'Alright. I'll pick it up tomorrow. I can also pop into O'Gorman's and buy that book for Anne Marie, what was it again?'

'*The Brothers Karamazov*!'

'Right.'

The next day Father, at his lunch break, walked up to Glynn's Toy Shop from the Hynes Building on St Augustine Street where he worked. I feel guilty thinking this, he mused, but, maybe that flippin' fluffy rabbit has been sold. Junior spotted it nearly ten days ago. Surely, some other kid in the whole of Connacht had his eye on that rabbit! If it's gone, it's gone. So be it. Let fate decide.

Father ascended to the second floor of Glynn's where the offending plaything had been posited. He looked around. It was no longer on the shelf! What relief. Problem solved. Bless you, fate. Can buy the boy some football boots. Or a sports kit. Or a rugby ball. Then he spotted Dinny Dooley, an old friend who worked in Glynn's, carrying a large box.

'Jeez. Howya Rory – me auld stock.'

'Howya Dinny. How's business?'

'Crazy. How's Bernie and the kids? In for some Christmas shopping?'

'Actually, I am. You wouldn't have any rugby balls here, would you?'

'Not our area. That would be Sports. Try Costello's. Anyway, all they want this year is this fella.'

Father heard some faint ringing as Dinny began to unpack the box. A box that contained ten sky blue fluffy rabbits. Dinny took one out and shook it.

'It's the bell that does it. All the five-year olds love that bell.'

Fate *had* decided. Father paused.

'They are rather cute,' he stated unconvincingly. 'I'll take one. Anne Marie might like one.'

Dinny looked surprised.

'Anne Marie? Are you sure? Last time I was talking to that young one, this time last year, she corrected me about Pythagoras's Theorem.'

'She's not all brains. She still likes her toys.'

Then father had an idea.

'But, she wouldn't like that bell. Do you know anyonc who could remove it? '

'Sure. Emily in the shop will do it for you. No problem. You can pick it up tomorrow.'

'Thanks, Dinny.'

Christmas morning arrived. Mother gave father a pair of socks and some Erinmore plug tobacco for his pipe. Father gave Mother some perfume. Anne Marie received three presents. In addition to *The Brothers Karamazov*, she received a book called *The Joys of Advanced Trigonometry* and the abridged works of Friedrich Schiller in German.

I received a transistor radio, a Leeds United soccer

scarf and a permanently mute sky blue fluffy rabbit with a scar from neck to belly that would have made a cardiologist blush.

THE COMEDY JUNKIE
(featuring Quasimodo O'Shaughnessy)

It is 1991. I am Quasimodo O'Shaughnessy. Stand-up comedian. The best thing about my act is my name. I am booked out of curiosity and rarely re-booked. The stage is not my home. It is more like a youth hostel in Prague. I never storm during my act. I just lightly rain shower. I refer to laughs as Godot. I spend most evenings waiting for one.

I live in London. They say a man who grows tired of London grows tired of life.

Zzzzzzzzzz.

Stuck in a dingy bedsit in Morden and deeply depressed about my non-burgeoning career, I develop a serious drugs problem – I can't afford any.

I want them. I need them. To forget who I am. (Like all the comedy agents I ring).

But where can I get my hands on some?

Desperate to partake in this dangerous snorty needle netherworld, I start hooking up with another comedian on the circuit, the well-connected and slightly dodgy X. (X is not his real first initial just in case fans of Xavier Burgess, obscure and justly neglected London-based Irish comedian think I'm referring to him). Me and X start taking E. And some blow. And some caine. Caine? Ok, initially, I don't completely master the lingo but almost immediately I feel a complete transformation in personality.

I imagine myself an airline pilot in a 1960s advertisement. Airborne. Confident. In control of my own destiny.

I also start wearing a slightly silly camp white-peaked cap.

This new confidence gives me the brio to constantly harangue venue managers and wangle gigs. Suddenly, I have work lined up. Once more. Now, all I have to do is be funny. Once more. Forget once more. Just once. Be funny once. That's all I ask. Be funny once.

My first newly arranged gig is in a place called The Laugh-A-Go-Go in East Croydon. Since artificial stimulants have helped me in the day-to-day business of my career, I start to wonder if they may also help me in the actual execution of my career. Look at George Carlin, Lenny Bruce, Richard Pryor – funny guys. The drugs helped open their minds to a new comedy frontier, ok with Lenny Bruce it became a sort of final frontier, and Richard Pryor had that unfortunate free-basing accident in 1982 (by this stage my lingo has become flawless) but in the greater scheme of things it did seem to clarify their artistic mission.

So the night of the gig, I decide, yes. I will, for the first time, take something before going on-stage.

I drop a few E's. On the ground. Outside the venue. They were my last E's. I go to retrieve them but a one-eyed, three-legged stray poodle has got to them first. *He's* going to have an unforgettable night. *He'll* be the funniest pooch, or feel like the funniest pooch in East Croydon, but what about me? I had to score some gear. Soon. I was on in thirty minutes.

Twenty of those minutes are spent standing at the back door of the bar, outside the Gents looking shifty, trying to attract the attention of various single men and getting punched. I come to the conclusion that this strategy isn't working and is causing an unnecessary loss of blood. I also decide to stop wearing that slightly silly camp white-peaked cap.

Three minutes to go. I am saved. She is pick-me-up gorgeous. An all-purpose comedy groupie with her own unique fashion sense. Punk Amish. She is in love with anything to do with comedy and anybody doing comedy. She recognizes me from a photo in *Time Out* from 1987 and asks me do I want to do a line. In my pre-lingo days and being originally from a modestly populated town in Ireland, I'd have thought she was suggesting we go steady, have a bit of relationship, maybe get married, have a couple of kids, who knows where it'll take us, but in my new found level of narcotics sophistication I know exactly what she means.

We retire to the ladies. She locks the door of the cubicle. She puts a line of cocaine on the rim of the loo. This is seedy, authentic, on-the-edge living.

But not very hygienic.

She snorts a line. She arranges one for me. Suddenly I hear the MC announce my name. I have to go. I half-snort some of the powder, get up, unlock the cubicle and somehow find myself on stage. I open my mouth. I sound like the electronically altered voice of a former satanic cult member on one of those television documentaries. After two minutes, I realize the drugs aren't opening any new comedy frontier. It is the same old comedy frontier. Only much less coherent.

And over the next excruciating fifteen minutes I don't hear one Godot.

HARD SHOULDER

I often wonder would I make a better pallbearer if I were born in America. Coffins are carried by the handles in America.

In Ireland they are carried on the shoulders.

I have very small shoulders.

This coupled with other ailments not particularly conducive to the transportation of a casket – dodgy hernia, tight upper trapezius muscles and my cervicogenic headaches – means I always stare at the ground when, post-funeral ceremony, help is requested for coffin-carrying duties.

However, being a member of a family, a tribe, a community, the older you get, as members of that family, tribe, and community die off, you are expected to step up and offer your assistance. Especially since those that have done the carrying are now doing the dying and need replacing.

But still I have always remained steadfast in my non-participation.

That is, until one funeral in April last year.

'Will you help carry the coffin?'

'No.'

'I think it would be the right thing to do.'

'I'd rather not. My tendonitis seems to have flared up.'

'But, it's your father.'

I had to think about this. Eldest son really should join in on the ritual. In all the books, all the movies, all the television news items, the eldest son is always visible, top right or top left, taking control, manfully suppressing tears and guiding that wooden box to its final destination.

What was wrong with me? Had I no shame?

Reluctantly, I joined my cousins. Masculine mountain men. Some looked Greek with their swarthy features and bountiful facial hair. We planned the first step of the manoeuvre. The successful lifting and conveying of coffin from inside the church to the hearse outside. All I remember is that things went very well for the first twenty seconds. Then blank.

I was later told I had fainted. When I came to, Lucy, my six-year old niece was offering me some ice cream on one of the pews as her brother, my fifteen-year old nephew Greg, had been drafted in to successfully move father's pine structure through the church door.

I never felt so humiliated. This will never happen again I vowed as I gently caressed my throbbing elbow. I have to get in shape. Next funeral, I will be first in line to offer help. I will carry the damn thing on my own! If needs be!

Over the next month I devised a strict fitness regime. On the exercise bike every morning. On the treadmill every evening. Every manner of stretch. I used weights. Bulked up. In six weeks I was a new man. Primed for any funeral service action. All I needed was the right opportunity.

I waited.

And waited.

But the months went by. Nobody died. Not one member of my extended family passed away. Uncle Ned was eighty-seven. Had been in a coma since November 2011, but he kept hanging in there. A medical aberration, one neurologist claimed. Auntie Flossie had had so many cancers we'd lost count. Her latest was a lump on the coccyx. Coccyx cancer. I'd never heard of that one. But she developed it. Yet she was a fighter. 'I'll beat this,' she kept saying. And strangely enough, I believed her. Grand-uncle Roger, ninety-two, crashed his Ford Cortina at top speed into a tree. The car was a complete write-off, but Roger emerged unscathed and just went out and bought himself a new Jaguar.

I was desperate. Those gym fees were stacking up and I wanted to prove my newfound casket-carrying credentials to my family. My tribe. My people. To keep myself readied, I even started going to random funeral services out of town, approaching mourners and saying 'Sorry for your loss. By the way, do you need any help to carry the coffin? Are you a man short?' They'd just look at me, slightly scared. 'No, thanks. Now. Go. Away. Please.'

Finally in early February, Uncle Ned, sadly, inevitably, passed away. If only I hadn't booked that holiday to Madeira. My girlfriend Gillian had been suggesting it for months. She liked my new shape and refined pectoral qualities but had felt I needed a break from my constant pallbearing ruminations.

A month later, however, my luck changed. Mother rang.

'Your Auntie Flossie died this morning.'

'Great. When's the funeral?'

My cousins were both impressed and surprised when I immediately approached them after the funeral mass. I told them I would consider it a great honour to help carry Flossie's coffin. They nodded. We started to lift it from the bier. I felt no problems whatsoever. No ligaments tweaked, no bones strained, and most important of all, no fainting. I was 100% fit and in peak shape. In fact, belatedly, I felt this sort of thing suited me. I was a natural. Nothing like good, honest, physical labour to make a man of you.

We effortlessly shifted the coffin out of the church and seamlessly navigating the church steps, headed towards the hearse outside. We gently placed the coffin in the back. There was a pause. I was feeling silently chuffed. At last, I finally belonged to my family. My tribe. My people. I envisaged future funerals. I'd always be there. Standing firm. A sturdy rock of dependability. Always available for any onerous chores.

Then cousin Fintan turned to me.

'My first one of those.'

'What do you mean?'

'Those eco-coffins. Cardboard. Flossie was a mad one for the environment. They only weigh a fraction of the normal ones.'

THE KARL MACDERMOTT ARCHIVE PART ONE

(A sample from the papers, correspondence and documents writer Karl MacDermott donated to the Glenamaddy Regional Technical and Business College in September 2017. The items were swiftly returned the following month.)

EXTRACT FROM UNPUBLISHED BOOK *THE EMERALD ALMANAC – A BOOK OF LITTLE KNOWN IRISH FACTS* – 2005

Nodding Etiquette: One of the things the intrepid traveller notices while travelling from the east coast of Ireland to the west coast of Ireland is the choreography of the nod. In the capital city, Dublin, one barely nods in acknowledgement at someone one knows vaguely but the further west one travels, nodding etiquette becomes more overstated and, one might add, extreme. By the time one gets to Galway, men are willing to slip discs in their neck to nod at you. In Galway, this is sometimes referred to as 'a head-butt of acquaintance'.

Most Informed Buttocks: It is a well-known historical fact that during the 1970s and early 1980s the buttocks of young Irish girls were the most well-read sets of buttocks in the whole of the western world. This was because when a young girl was in school, her teachers, the nuns, would say to her 'if a boy wants you to sit on his lap you must place a newspaper between your bottom and the boy.' As a result, a generation of young female behinds became extremely well informed on major world events like the oil crises of 1973, Richard Nixon's decline and fall with the Watergate investigations of 1974 and the previously mentioned young rears also became knowledgeable on less earth shattering, more parochial events like the Fianna Fáil landslide election victory of 1977 and the Johnny Logan Eurovision Song Contest victory of 1980.

The Inner Yelper: Most Irish people face an eternal struggle. The conflict between the outward sophisticate and the inner yelper. The post-1970s outward sophisticate has attempted to reject his country's musical heritage over a lifetime. Give him the urban blues of Chicago, the sweet soul sound of Detroit, west coast jazz, psychedelic folk rock and Jamaican reggae. Not Planxty. But when he steps into a bar in Doolin one evening and hears three bearded bowsies pick up a fiddle, a flute and a bodhrán, a profound unrest starts rumbling within him. He starts to involuntarily move his right knee to the hated diddle-dei. Feels all epileptic and jerky. He tries to restrain himself. He even visits the pub toilet and has a talk with himself in the mirror. 'Stop this right now! You are embarrassing me.' But when he returns and sits down, the same turmoil persists. He is filled with self-loathing and disgust. His face contorts and he punches himself in the ribs as he feels the first yelp coming on. He has tried to control himself but cannot any longer, as if, from the bowels of his ancestors, one of the loudest yelps is heard this side of Ennistymon. Yeeeowwww! He hits himself on the head but is now in a frenzy. It is pointless. Another yelp. Yeeeowwww! His inner yelper has been unleashed – damned inner yelper – and another night of shame has arrived.

The Irish Pharmacy: On my wide-ranging travels I have often marvelled at how swift and easy it is to get a prescription filled in the pharmacies of other European countries. For example, in Germany, a customer enters the pharmacy with a prescription. The prescription is taken by the pharmacist. The pharmacist goes over to a wall of drawers. Finds the appropriate medication or tablets. Places them in a paper bag. Charges the customer, then hands customer the paper bag. The whole transaction takes no more than two minutes. However, in Ireland things are not so simple. A visit to an Irish pharmacy is a perplexing, time-consuming and ultimately draining affair. The customer enters with a prescription. The prescription is handed over to the person behind the counter. But the person behind the counter is not the person who deals with the prescription. The person behind the counter is usually a family member with only the slightest connection to the whole pharmacology universe. The person behind the counter yawns, then takes the prescription, turns around and hands it over to one of the pharmacists. That pharmacist looks at the prescription and then starts to confer with *another* pharmacist. The customer becomes slightly paranoid as both pharmacists begin to whisper conspiratorially. In Ireland, this is known as the 'pharmacist huddle'. The whispers continue interminably and finally the second pharmacist takes the prescription and goes behind what is generally referred to in the world of Irish apothecary as 'the curtain of intrigue'. Great thinkers, sociologists and scientists have been baffled over the decades as to what exactly goes on behind 'the curtain of intrigue'. And why it takes such a very long time to fill out a modest prescription. The customer waits. And waits. And waits. Anxiety increases. Not an ideal scenario for those customers seeking a prescription for anti-anxiety medication. The waiting continues. The pharmacist remains behind the 'curtain of intrigue' seemingly forever lost in that pharma-den of mystery. After eleven minutes the pharmacist reappears with a paper bag and in a business-like manner calls out the customer's name. The paper bag is charged for and, as an afterthought, the pharmacist tells the customer that the exact medication the customer was looking for was unavailable but what is in the paper bag is *almost* exactly the same. The customer considers querying this, but being beyond weary and exhausted at this stage, just pays for the medication, takes the paper bag and rapidly exits the pharmacy.

Joyful Days at the Beach: The Irish love to drive to the beach. But unlike the populace of most other nations once they get to the beach they don't actually leave their car. They prefer to remain seated and just stare. A nation not of sea voyagers, but of sea voyeurs, happily static behind their windscreens and parked next to similar stay-rooted-in-their-car enthusiasts. After three hours of staring, sleeping, snoring and re-reading the previous Sundays' newspaper, a flask is retrieved from under the car seat. Metallic milky sweet tea is poured into a plastic lid and, with that first sip, a kind of mundane nirvana is achieved.

EXTRACT FROM AN UNPUBLISHED GALWAY MEMOIR *THE FELLAS YOU'D SEE AROUND* – 2007

There was this guy in Galway years ago, known as the fuck off guy. He was sort of a drunk, a vagrant and if you looked at him and he looked at you, he'd tell you to fuck off. Sometimes you didn't even have to look at him but if he was within earshot of you, he'd still tell you to fuck off. People would say 'keep well away from that fella or he'll tell you to fuck off.' So one day I'm strolling down Mainguard Street, lost in thoughts, I look up and he is right there in front of me. That happens sometimes with drunks. They just appear like some hygienically challenged burping apparition. So I stare at the fuck off guy and he stares at me. I think, ok, I'll wait for it, get it over with. But there is just a pause. He says nothing. He merely looks at me with a slight pity in his eyes. And then walks by. Oddly, I feel sort of cheated. He spends his whole life saying fuck off to everyone from as far south as Ballyvaughan to as far north as Crossmolina, but he doesn't say it to me. So, I chase after him and I say 'hey wait a minute fuck off guy – you say fuck off to everyone else but you didn't say fuck off to me, why not?' And he looks at me and then he just says lowly 'fuck off.' I say 'thanks, that's all I was looking for, I'll let you be on your way.' I walk down the road a bit and I hear him scream 'Fuck Off!' to somebody else further across the street and I think he didn't give the fuck off he said to me that level of aggression. It was sort of throw away. Resigned. Distinctly low energy. It wasn't really a fuck off. It was jaded. I mean, if he's going to say fuck off to me he has to do it the right way otherwise what's the point! So I run up the road after him. I even tap him on the shoulder and to do that to the fuck off guy, I mean, think about it, if that doesn't get the necessary aggression, what will? So he turns around and looks at me. Long pause. 'You again.' I'm gob-smacked. The fuck off guy has a vocabulary of *four* words. I explain the situation. I wasn't happy with his fuck off. Why should I be treated differently? He just shrugs his shoulders and walks away.

Fast forward twenty years. I'm walking up Eglington Street and I see the fuck off guy. I won't deny that I haven't had the odd sleepless night in the last two decades mulling over what happened between us. A man doesn't forget something like that in a hurry. The fact of being singled out for a lesser 'fuck off.' I'm going to settle this once and for all. I decide to cross the street and approach him. I have to admit he has aged well. All those years of napalming his liver with god knows what and living the life of an abusive hobo – he doesn't look too bad! He's almost a walking advertisement for that sort of life. I approach him and just before I am about to introduce myself, he turns around, faces me and with an extreme ferocity bellows 'Jesus loves you!' I sigh sadly and walk away. I briefly enter a Proustian daydream on how everything passes, on how eras end, how local characters and local areas change. Nothing is constant in this impermanent world. The fuck off guy is no more. He is now the Jesus loves you guy. My reverie is rudely interrupted as 'Jesus loves you!' is howled once more further down the road.

EXTRACT FROM UNPUBLISHED POETRY COLLECTION *A LOT OF WHITE ON THE PAGE* – 2014

A Poem with the Word Cancer in the Title

In avoiding people you know who have cancer
You acquire the nimble dexterity of a dancer
Leaping as you cross the street
To escape that awkward meet
And charging on ahead like a Bengal lancer.

Don't Try This At Home

There was man from Lancashire
Who injected his mouth with Ecstasy
E by gum.

One Arty Lady

She liked to smear her breasts in honey and jello
She once was in a play by Pirandello
She told me she played the oboe or was it the cello?
She always read Roth but didn't like Bellow
She was one arty lady.

Reflections on a Dead Hollywood Star

If River Phoenix had lived
And he'd had kids
And they'd grown up
What would they have called him?
The old man, River?

Brief Poem Number 18

The world is a funny place
There is Paris
And there is Naas.

Starry Starry Night

Vincent Van Gogh
Knew his way around
Because he always had
That one ear to the ground.

Red Hurley is Doing a Gig at The Red Cow Inn

You are born. You grow up a bit. You watch some telly. Music shows with cheap sets. And there he is – for the first time – Red Hurley. Presenter Thelma Mansfield announces he'll be doing a gig at The Red Cow Inn.

You're a teenager. You hang around town. You're known as Swaggerwank. You have attitude. You drink cans of beer and shout aggressively at empty phone-boxes. Walking home late at night you see a poster – Red Hurley is doing a gig at The Red Cow Inn.

You go to college. You travel on a J-1 Visa. You see the Grand Canyon. You get laid. You come back to Ireland. You're walking down the street. You see a poster – Red Hurley is doing a gig at The Red Cow Inn.

You finish your degree. You go to Australia. You get a job. After three years you come home to visit. You've become obsessed with staying fit. One evening you're jogging down the street. You notice something – Red Hurley is doing a gig at The Red Cow Inn.

The years roll on. You move to London. You have a career in logistics. You get married. You lose your hair. You have a son. Your parents are getting old. You fly to Dublin to see them. You're walking down the street. On the side of a bus you spot an advertisement – Red Hurley is doing a gig at The Red Cow Inn.

Your marriage breaks up. You have a mid-life crisis. You do something daft. You join Boko Haram. You immediately know you've made a dreadful mistake. You get out of Africa. Catch a connecting flight from Luton and arrive in Dublin. Sitting in a cab, you look out the window and glimpse a poster – Red Hurley is doing a gig at The Red Cow Inn.

You want to expand your horizons. Fifty is the new thirty. You train to become an astronaut. You are hired for a mission and become the first Irishman in space. You travel to Jupiter. You realize how insignificant you are and what a vast amazing universe surrounds us. You come back to earth. After crash landing in the Indian Ocean they keep you in a special decontaminating facility for eighteen months and then fly you home specially. There is a civic reception for you. You stand on a platform in College Green and wave to the crowd but out of the corner of your eye you spot something – a poster – Red Hurley is doing a gig at The Red Cow Inn.

Your parents die. Your son is in IT. You've a new relationship in Brighton with a life coach called Tundra. She makes you very happy. She'd love to see Ireland, so you go one day, but on your first night in Dublin you don't feel well. Turns out you have major heart problems. And possibly cancer. And a definite brain hemorrhage with a stroke thrown in for good measure. They have to rush you to the hospital. You're lying down in the back of an ambulance. Tundra holds your hand and two male nurses look on. Stuck in traffic one asks the other 'Conor, have you anything lined up for the anniversary on Friday?' 'Yeh. Meal at seven. A few drinks. Then we're off to see Red Hurley at The Red Cow Inn.'

PRACTICING MINDFULNESS BEFORE ANOTHER MEETING WITH SISYPHUS

It is breakfast-time. Living in the moment. I am now listening to some beautiful Brazilian guitar artistry by Antonio Carlos Jobim. I am now cherishing the gulp of this strong and satisfying cup of coffee. Cherish the gulp. A sublimely executed gulp. I am now placing the cup of coffee on the table. I am looking at the stain on the kitchen wall under the clock. It is a beautiful stain. Shaped like a heart. A big heart full of endless love. Chew on the last piece of bread. Roll it around my mouth. Taste the sour dough. Feel the food go down the gullet. Swallow. A sublimely executed swallow followed by yet another sublimely executed gulp. I pick up the empty dishes, cup and dirty cutlery from the table and walk over to the sink. I enjoy the sensation of turning on the tap. And have a sense of wonder as the flowing water mixed with a modest squirt of washing-up liquid and some mild scrubbing results in the dishes being cleaned. I now propel myself in a forward-like motion up the stairs, cherish the feel of the wooden floor under my feet and I arrive on the landing. I am going over to close the window in the bed-room, as it is getting rather windy. I marvel at the strength of that breeze. Yes. Marvel at the breeze. I must now evacuate my bowels. Enjoy the physical release of the bowel movement, am awed by the bowel movement, another exquisitely executed bowel movement. I wipe my rectum with toilet paper, feel the toilet paper on the rectum, enjoy without being overly concerned, as after all the rectum is an erogenous zone and it is perfectly normal and ok to cherish the sensation of a good rectum wipe. A perfectly executed rectum wipe. I notice the slight spot of blood on the toilet paper. Think of my mother, when years ago she had applied too much red lipstick on her lips she would chomp lightly on a piece of tissue and leave a red stain. The colour and shape of mother's lipstick on the tissue is similar to the colour and shape of hemorrhoid blood on the toilet paper. From my mother's mouth to my anus. An interesting and strange connection. Is it a perverse connection? No, it is just a thought. And I will be non-judgmental regarding that thought. I will not consider it an evil thought, a squalid thought or a disgusting thought. Just a thought. It is not a fact. My mother's mouth is not my anus. It is just a thought. Like a cloud passing by. Thoughts are not facts. As I pull up my trousers and listen attentively to the eruption of the toilet flush, I think of that old Hollywood joke – 'What do hemorrhoids and awards have in common?' 'Sooner or later every asshole gets one.' Too true. Even I got one, and each day I must be thankful for that, however obscure, Nora Barnacle Anything To Do With Galway Literary Award 2001.

Think about my meeting with Sisyphus. I will tell

him I've been practicing mindfulness while contemplating his book idea. But that is in the immediate future and mindfulness is about embracing and caressing the present. Becoming aware of my every sense. Live in the moment. Breathe in. Breathe out. I whisper my mantra softly. It echoes in my head. *This is your now. This is your now.*

I leave the house and lock the door. I treasure the jangle of my house keys in my coat pocket and I cross the road and arrive at a bus stop. I wait for a bus. Cherish the waiting. Enjoy the rain. Be astounded by the rain. All those raindrops. Enjoy the feeling of getting wet. The persistent rain falls on my cheek. The cars go by. I get splashed by a car. I don't scream. Yes. The driver is not a complete insensitive ignoramus. There is probably a very good reason for his unnecessary speed. Maybe he is rushing his pregnant wife to the hospital. No, he was alone. Ok. Maybe he is rushing home to pick her up to bring her to the hospital. Yes. He has his reasons. I don't hate him. Or any of the other drivers. I love them. I want to embrace them. We are all in this carnival of chaos together. And most of us spend our allotted time doing the best we can. A state of serenity descends upon me. Still waiting for the bus. I listen to my breathing. I repeat my mantra. *This is your now. This is your now.* The bus still doesn't arrive. *This is your now*. I try a new mantra. *I am my only me. I am my only me*. Try another one. *I love me who is my only me*. And another one. *I love my only me who is me*. Two council workmen suddenly appear and start to spray footpath cleaning chemicals at the bus stop. *My* bus stop. I am staying calm. Still loving my only me. I am admiring their yellow florescent work-jackets as they spray. I breathe in the spray. Noxious toxins. What are they spraying? Agent Orange? They are just doing their job. But did they have to turn up at the bus stop I was waiting at? Now I can't position myself next to the bus stop because they are there but if a bus arrives, and I'm not standing at the bus stop it will just drive by. Stupid confounded council workmen! I suddenly notice this approaching vortex of agitation. Stop this! I am veering towards corrosive negativity and must re-direct my thoughts! But I am finding it quite difficult! These council workmen are bothering me. All council workmen do. And their ridiculous cleaning vehicles they drive on the footpath that knock every one out of the way. Do they actually make anything cleaner? Stop this! *I am my only me who I love, I am my only me who I love...* Or do these machines just create noise and mayhem. What a badly run city to live in. And the potholes, don't get me started on the potholes, you can't step anywhere without twisting an ankle. Hold it right there brain! Stop all this negativity! *This is your now. I am here now. I love me who is in the now.* The bus. Here comes the bus. I am yards from the stop and I'll have to flag it down. Yes. Stop, Mr Bus Driver. It's your job. You are a bus driver. You see people at a bus stop. You stop. Thank you. I get on the bus. Tell the driver my destination. Place my Leap Card on the allotted space. His machine takes an age reading it. I breathe in and breathe out. Finally I'm allowed pass. Walk towards a vacant seat. I calm down as I sit. Feel the seat underneath me. It is reasonably new. Nice fibre and texture. Not too worn. It is a nice seat. No need to dwell on whatever state of trousers has sat on this seat before. This morning. Yesterday. Last week. The jetsam and the jetsam. No, concentrate on the positives. All the junkies now use the Luas Red Line. For free. Yes. No more junkies on your bus route. Junkies walk as if they are walking against a very strong wind. Except there is no wind. How *do* junkies defy gravity? If junkies had been out in Isaac Newton's time, the future of scientific discovery may have turned out differently. Yes. But I am mentally digressing once more. Come back to the wellness zone. Re-enter the wellness zone. Concentrate on the positives. Breathe in. Breathe out. *This is your now. I am my only me. I love me who is my only me.* Cherish sitting on the seat. Notice the splendour of the raindrops on the window. The random patterns they make. Repeat your mantra. *This is your now.* Free your mind before that meeting with Sisyphus. Attempt another mindfulness exercise. Try to breathe into your toe. It proves as difficult as it sounds. Try again. No. Still doesn't work. Maybe if I wear a different pair of socks? Will get back to it later. Ponder matters as the bus stops at some traffic lights. Ruminate on double decker buses and their mirroring of life's stages. (If one is a non-driver). From the age of four to ten you sit downstairs in the double decker bus. With a parent or relative. From the age of ten when you are on the bus on your own or with school pals, you venture upstairs and go to the very front of the bus. Thrilled by the aerial panoramic view of the world. Granted not the world. Salthill. That sun-free seaside resort in the West of Ireland where the wind always decapitates your recently purchased ice-cream cone. Up until your twenties, you love that front window upstairs on the bus. Then you think, ok I've done the front of the bus thing enough, I can sit in the middle of the upper deck. But you're still embracing life and danger and still going up those stairs! You enjoy the energy and the vibrancy of the upper deck. The good-looking young office workers, the boisterous schoolboys (were you not one yourself?), the chatter and sweet mayhem of life. But gradually everything passes. Somewhere around your fortieth birthday you are not as charmed by the upper deck any longer. The background noise of humanity has started to bother you. The office workers are talking mindlessly and interminably on their smart phones, the schoolboys have become less boisterous but more sinister and uncouth, and of course the odd misfit, long term tenants of the upper deck, drool and stare at you from the seat across the aisle and incoherently ask you what time it is. Then on or around your forty-eighth birthday after a particularly perilous descent, you think maybe you should stay downstairs from now on. Return to where it all began. Bringing it all back home. Sitting with the old dears and their smell of hairspray and stale urine and their look of quiet panic. Or being squashed by the obese gentleman with a beer gut the size of a rhino's bottom. Ah yes. Life's full circle on that double decker bus. My bus reverie suddenly shatters. I hear my smartphone ring. Number unknown. I take the call. I can face all adversity. *This is your now*. It is Fidelma. She tells me Sisyphus is very busy at the moment and wants to defer our appointment. I am a little disappointed but think of all the good things he has done for my career. None. Now, I'm even more disappointed. And angry. I feel anger. Intense anger. *This is your now. This is your now*. I temporarily succeed in banishing my disappointed feelings and as I thank her for letting me know, my anger subsides. She then tells me Sisyphus still hasn't got round to reading those first three stories I gave him a few weeks back (nearly two months, don't think I'm not counting, and I gave him in total, six stories, not three, six stories) but he has given them to her – a part-time reader for Sludge Lagoon Press – and she promises me she'll read them over the weekend when Sisyphus is away visiting his sister in Tubbercurry. I take a deep breath, again. *I am my only me who I happen to love who is me. I am my only me who I happen to love who is me*. I tell her there is no hurry and that I look forward to hearing her opinion of the stories when I meet Sisyphus next. The phone call ends. I slowly develop pounding palpitations and my anger slowly rises again. It is still raining. The bus remains rooted in traffic. A headache is evolving. That toothache in my brain feeling. I devise a new mantra. *The pointlessness of mindfulness. The pointlessness of mindfulness. The pointlessness of mindfulness.*

THREE STORIES ON A MEMORY STICK MISPLACED AFTER KARL'S PHONE CALL WITH FIDELMA

THE LOST DIARY OF EVA BRAUN

(In our continuing series of extracts from the recently discovered diaries of Eva Braun, we look at an entry from March 11th, 1938)

Things came to a head today at the Berghof. Adolfchen turns up with some of his guys at about midday. I finally make a stand. I insist they take off their jackboots before coming in. Ulrike had just cleaned the new Scandinavian Pine floor and I was damned if those boys were just going to swan in. God knows what they get up to wearing those jackboots. I know, it's all for the good of the Fatherland, the thousand year Reich etcetera, etcetera, etcetera, but hygienically it doesn't bear thinking about.

Adolfchen hits the roof. He insists that no member of the party, whether lowly Stormtrooper or Waffen SS, should be asked to remove their jackboots when entering the house. Frankly, he feels it's unmanly to have to step into those leather *Hausschuhe* I had specially made in Pirmasens, but for me this is a point of principle. I refuse to back down.

Adolfchen then starts screaming histrionically. Save it for those party congresses, I think. Such a drama queen. He says they have this big meeting planned today to discuss strategies towards Sudetenland (should they annex now or later) and here we are getting side tracked by debates about household hygiene and footwear! I look at him calmly. I run this house, I tell him, and we have to have some basic rules and one of those rules is, when you come through that door, the shoes come off!

The others start getting embarrassed. Himmler clears his throat. Its ok, Führer, we'll take off the jackboots, no problem. There's no strop from Von Ribbentrop. Even Goering is completely malleable as he flirts with Ulrike when she presents him with the guest *Hausschuhe*.

There is a long pause. They stand around and look over at Adolfchen who remains stationary by the window. He is still wearing his jackboots. He looks so agonized. So forlorn. He looks like he may cry at any moment. I feel an overwhelming desire to go over, take him in my arms and hug him, but some things are more important than sentiment. Like a spotless house!

Finally, my Adolfchen acquiesces and removes his jackboots. I run over to a cupboard and take out the special gold embossed pair of *Hausschuhe* graced with a black swastika on each foot. Ulrike picks up all the jackboots and deposits them at the front porch.

The tension between us persists during dinner. It didn't help that I still haven't mastered couscous. The

German *Hausfrau* was not put on this earth to serve her man vegetarian dishes!

Later Adolfchen is in his study. I approach tentatively. What are you doing, *mein Liebling*? He tells me he has to choose the shirt colours for some of the newer fascist organizations in Europe, but that the Icelandic fascists, The Polka Dot Shirts aren't happy. I ask him, did he like his gold embossed *Hausschuhe*. He sighs. I leave him be. I ponder that all relationships have these small moments of friction and decide to defer until tomorrow broaching the on-going issue of trimmed moustache hair in the bathroom sink.

CARRY ON DOCTOR

It's the week before Christmas 1984. I'm romantically interested in a med student called Maeve and I've tried over the previous month to initiate some minimal physical contact with her. Her response seems best described as non-committal. The question remains, does she fancy me? I have always been dreadful at reading signals in this, the minefield matters of the heart. Trawling for positives, she *has* grabbed hold of my hand once, but proviso alert, it was up the Twelve Bens during that foggy and slippery day out with the Mountaineering Society. But now, a more positive definitive sign may be in the offing. She is going home for Christmas on Thursday but before doing so, she has suggested we have a small dinner with some wine in her flat on Whitestrand Avenue on Wednesday night. Her flatmate will be out. We will have the place to ourselves. We can relax and talk. I'm thrilled. Excited. A little anxious.

Wednesday arrives. I have had a very light supper. I am sitting on the sofa of my living-room at seven o'clock. *Carry on Doctor* has just started on the television and my father is watching it. I look over at him. I think to myself he is fifty now. He is past it. He is all washed up. World be prepared! It's my time now, baby! My time now! Yes. My time now. I rock gently in anticipation.

My father laughs at Kenneth Williams. I am unable

to concentrate on what mayhem Jim Dale, Joan Sims and Hattie Jacques are creating because I am pre-occupied with having to time my exit. I must depart the house at quarter-past-seven to be at Whitestrand Avenue at seven-thirty. For *un diner pour deux*. A rendezvous where Maeve will cook the dinner and I will supply the wine. I exhale weakly and hope my father won't notice the stolen bottle of Liebfraumilch from his wine cellar (sounds better than scullery) secretly packed in my rucksack in the hallway.

Charles Hawtrey has just made an appearance, when I stand up and announce I am going out. 'Where to?' my father asks. 'Friends.' I reply vaguely. 'Well, before you go out – don't forget to take in the bin.'

'Nineteen years old and still having to take in the bin! You're past it, old man! It's my time now, baby!'

I quickly put on my purple anorak, grab the rucksack and exit the front door. I walk out the gate and stare at the bin. Will I just leave it? I decide the revolution can wait. I take in the bin. Fuelled by a nervous energy, I stride purposefully down Dr Mannix Road. Vistas of the future open out ahead of me. Many futures. Many roads. My time now, baby, I think, my time now.

Doubt momentarily enters my mind. Will she like Liebfraumilch? Maybe she's a wine snob. No, it's ok. She's from Tuam. But more importantly, will there be any post-prandial Carry On with this future Doctor? And if so, am I meant to make the first move? How can I make the first move if I'm sitting across a table from her? Or on a couch with a plate of food on my lap? What happens if I can't finish her chicken fricassee? Oh shit, I forgot to gargle with Listerine.

At twenty-nine minutes past seven I am standing outside her front door. I wait for fifty-four seconds and then ring the bell. I am surprised to see her flatmate Fiona answer the door. 'Is Maeve there?' I ask. 'No, no, one of the lads from her class was going her way, and she decided to take a lift home early for Christmas. She apologises but says she'll definitely have you over for a bite to eat in the New Year.'

A bite to eat? A bite to eat?! The words do a Keith Moon in my ear-drums as it starts to rain. Whatever happened to the small dinner with some wine? She changed her mind. That's it! Or probably got back together with her old boyfriend, Austin, at the Mountaineering Society Christmas party! Austin, who studies Law, from Taylor's Hill. His daddy, a high-flying business executive, probably has two wine cellars! In *real* cellars!

I get very wet on the way home. When I finally arrive in the house I sneak in the back door and quickly return the purloined bottle of Liebfraumilch.

It is eight o'clock. I've changed out of my wet trousers. I walk into the living-room. I sit where I had been sitting. Sid James is ogling Barbara Windsor's breasts. I groan. 'Oh, you're back', my father says. 'Well that wasn't very long, was it? Who are those friends of yours, anyway?' 'Change of plan.' I say. There is a pause. 'Did you take in the bin?' I nod. I look at him again. I think of all the nights. When I come out of the toilet at three o'clock in the morning. No flushing. Night time rules. I see him on the landing. Approaching. Yellow pyjamas. Hair all askew. Small pot belly on view. He passes me as he needs to go too. His power eroding all the time. Fifty now and counting. He's past it. He's all washed up. World, be prepared! It's my time now, baby. My time now.

Just not tonight.

TRIP TO MOYNALTY
(Featuring Quasimodo O'Shaughnessy)

There's always some travel guy writing some travel thing about somewhere. About the places you've been or don't want to be. The places you've seen or don't want to see. Or the places you've died. Yes, dying. Stock in trade for a gag and bone man like myself. I was a comedian once. Ever hear of Quasimodo O'Shaughnessy? Thought not. Nobody else did either. That was the trouble. But there is this one gig that always sticks in my mind and makes the four hairs on my alopecia totalis cranium still stand up.

The time. Winter 1994. The place. Begorrah. Begob. Bejaysus. Be the hokey. Moynalty, Co. Meath. To pay a long deferred visit to my mother's reclusive bachelor uncle, Timmy Tommy. One night, I'm in Ugh's, the local bar. Proprietor's name was Hugh. Hadn't replaced the 'H' over the front door since 1968. Some guy comes up to me. 73% Ned Beatty. 27% Stacy Keach.

'Are you the comedian? Are ya?'

'Yeh.'

'Making people laugh must be the hardest job in the world.'

'It's the second hardest. Tracking hurricanes is harder.'

'Tell us a joke.'

I want Ned Stacy to go away. I pick one of my old ones that never got a laugh.

'Saint Paul was a great rugby player. People still talk about that conversion on the road to Damascus.'

He pauses, then starts to grin like a madman.

'More GAA country 'round here but Jaynee macker, not bad at all. You could be just the man I'm looking for! Would you like to make a few bob?'

The house is up a hill. Over a meadow. Through a bog. Under an unsettled blackcurrant sky. An Irish picture postcard designed by Edvard Munch. Ned Stacy wants me to entertain a 'small social gathering'. I surprise myself by agreeing immediately. Maybe because uncle Timmy Tommy, a true taciturn Meath man, and myself had run out of things to talk about after five minutes. My journey. My mother. The weather.

We arrive at the house on the hill. Introduced to a Virgie, 54 % Kathy Bates. 46% Elsa Lancaster. And Bartley, 78% Ernest Borgnine. 22% Charles Bronson. Virgie is odd. Bartley is scary.

'I brought the funnyman,' Ned Stacy announces.

'Will we bring him inside?' Virgie wonders.

'Sure, that's what he's here for,' Bartley growls in a register four levels lower than gravel-voiced.

I am ushered into a large back room. Dimly lit. Seems pretty cluttered. Is that furniture in the middle? No. A piano. Wrong again. It's a coffin. Oh. Next to another coffin.

Ned Stacy looks down, makes more introductions.

'Paddy Joe and Philomena Grimes.'

Paddy Joe, 93% Tom Courtney. Obviously a dead Tom Courtney. And Philomena. How can I put this? She looks quite unlike anybody I've ever seen in my life. Ned Stacy shakes his head.

'Their first holiday away, in Torremolinos, and aren't they run over by a tour bus. Took an age to bring them home.'

Bartley finally clears his gravel and speaks.

'Paddy Joe and my sister always loved a good laugh. A good joke.'

So Bartley is the brother. I scrutinize Philomena again. Yes. On second thoughts an uncanny family resemblance. Think Borgnine. With a perm. In a dress. Holding rosary beads.

Ned Stacy stops picking his nose.

'We were wondering. Given the night that's in it. Us here, having a bit of a wake, before we put them in the ground tomorrow, could you tell them an auld joke, ah go on, they loved a bit of a laugh!'

Virgie taps me on the shoulder.

'Go on there now! We'll see if you're any good at all!'

The other two start to laugh. Virgie joins in. Sometimes laughter in unison can create a certain warmth. A joint frivolous giddiness that announces it is good to be alive. This wasn't one of those times. I look down on Paddy Joe and Philomena.

Bartley stares at me. 'Tell them a joke. See if you can bring a smile to their lips. One last time.'

Suddenly I feel an upping of the ante. Doing London's Comedy Store in March 1989 – my only appearance – was less pressure.

A joke. Which one? What do I do?

Then an idea. There's an old habit in comedy. If you play in a small room with a strange audience, ideal time to try out some new material. And this was a small room with a strange audience. Very strange. Although maybe not the right crowd for my 'Mother Teresa – Secret Breakdancing Champion!' routine. Bartley glares. He is getting impatient. A pinball machine starts up in my chest. Must do something. My Padre Pio joke! Always works in Glasgow.

'Padre Pio, might have been a saint, but he always cheated at hide and seek.' I place my open palms over my eyes. There is a long pause. I start explaining. Always death for a comedian.

'See, he had the stigmata in the hands... allegedly.'

Ned Stacy gets it. He nods. But he's already a fan. Bartley and Virgie are unimpressed. I keep explaining.

'The holes. He could peek through the holes...'

This is becoming extremely uncomfortable.

'When he is counting. Hide and seek... one... two... three... he looks through his palms...'

Bartley's fist tightens. He is about to strike me when we hear the faintest titters emanating from the coffins.

Bartley and Virgie are stunned. Virgie blurts out.

'They laughed. Jesus, Mary, Joseph and the donkey, they laughed. Thank you so much. You made them laugh one last time.'

My face freezes. Not gobsmacked. Gobwhipped.

Walking back to Ugh's. Over the meadow. Through the bog. Still stunned. I turn to Ned Stacy.

'Well, that's something for my CV. Makes the dead laugh.'

He looks at me.

'I was starting to feel sorry for you back there. Used to be in show business myself years ago. Did a bit of an auld ventriloquist act. Mattie and the Dummy. Well, are you going to thank me or what?'

KARL SPEAKS AT THE CHARLIE AND THE CONTENDERS EVENING

(Each Wednesday evening in an upstairs room of a bar in Dublin 8, a group of show business and artistic underachievers gather and recount stories of what-might-have-been. The evening is called The Charlie and The Contenders Evening after the famous Marlon Brando scene from *On The Waterfront*. Karl spoke before the launch of a Charlie and The Contenders Writers Chapbook in which one of his stories was included.)

Good evening, all you no-hopers, embittered wrecks, setback connoisseurs and delusion facilitators, my name is Karl and this is my Charlie and The Contenders story. After I won the Nora Barnacle Anything To Do With Galway Literary Award in early 2001, I was a little hot, well not hot, lukewarm, ok not lukewarm, tepid. Riding the crest of a wave, ok, not a wave, a modestly sized ripple, but there was a certain interest from London. Irish writers were always popular over there. They find us so mystical and lyrical and Celtic and they are amazed we all want to smear our face with the clay of the place where our people are buried. Allegedly. Anyway, I sent the manuscript of my then new novel *The Irrelevant Playthings of a Cosmic Giant* to uh, Quentin Talisman of The QT Talent Agency. Big shot in Covent Garden. My own agent Sisyphus O'Shea was small scale. On reflection that's an insult to the expression 'small scale'. He was a termite in an industry of giants, and I wanted to be amongst the giants. Anyway, one Friday morning in May, about six weeks after I sent over my manuscript – unsolicited mind you, unsolicited – Quentin Talisman himself emails me. I can still recall the email verbatim. Ver-fucking-batim.

'I love this manuscript. I feel so good about this. Gemma, one of my interns, rescued it from the slush pile. I have a hunch about this one. Obviously, it will need some work and some judicious pruning but I want to represent you. I'll ring your number Monday morning.'

First thing I did, after a fifteen-minute caterwaul of triumph, was pop open a bottle of bubbly. Immediately, the open bottle of bubbly popped out of my hands. Delirious excitement equals slippery fingers. I didn't mind, though. Along with Bruce Springsteen, Barcelona and Netflix, I've always felt champagne is one of the more over-rated things on the planet. After a hurried clean-up and an unfortunate bloodied mash-up of my right forefinger and some shattered glass, that afternoon I ring my friend Alan to source some *real* drink. We go on an almighty bender. I remind Alan that this is no ordinary agent – this is Quentin Talisman, founder of the to-be-feared world famous QT Talent Agency. With offices in Hong Kong, Sydney and New York. No longer amongst the termites.

I have a dreadful hangover for three days. But it is worth every minute of it. And then I wait. Wait for Quentin. The Monday comes and goes. No contact from Quentin. A few more days pass. Still no call. I don't panic. Just yet. I'll give him a week. He is a busy man. A very successful globetrotting dynamo of the book trade. The following week arrives. Will I try and ring Quentin? No. Don't want to be too pushy. Or *desperate*. I'll leave it for a day or two. I'm happy with my decision. These things take time I tell myself as I have a cup of coffee in a local coffee shop. In the coffee shop I flick through the previous days' *Guardian*. I spot a headline. 'Top literary agent killed in a mysterious shooting incident last week.' I close my eyes. Stop catastrophizing, I tell myself. Stop catastrophizing. There are thousands of top literary agents in the UK. What are the chances? I open my eyes and read on. What are the chances?! Famous last words for my literary dreams! It *is* QT. My initial feeling of being proved right, again, a sort of smug self-righteousness I call 'vindicated catastrophizing' is immediately replaced by a feeling of mute howling terror. I ring Alan. Another bender. This time the hangover feels much worse.

The months go by. There is disruption and trauma at the offices of The QT Talent Agency. I wonder should I ring to see where I stand. How much time should I wait? Can't risk pressing my case too soon after the tragic and bizarre demise (a 17th century musket was involved) of the inestimable QT.

After five more weeks, I pluck up the courage and ring The QT Talent Agency. A Carole tells me that an Amanda has 'just stepped out of the office' but will ring me back in ten minutes. The minutes pass. The hours pass. The days pass. Amanda hasn't called back. I ring again. Amanda is at a meeting, will ring afterwards I am soothingly reassured by Carole. The minutes pass. The hours pass. The days pass. I'm starting to feel like a demented crank caller. A heavy breather. A drooler. The following Monday I ring again. An apologetic Carole says something like 'Amanda and yourself seem to keep missing each other.' End-of-my-tether me could have replied 'No, Amanda and myself don't keep missing each other. That would infer that Amanda has tried to contact me when I am unavailable to take the call, which is highly unlikely because I'm always available to take a call. If I'm not at home which I almost always am *because I don't have a life* she could always try to ring me on my mobile number which I have passed on to you, twice now, Carole. But in all those weeks since I've tried ringing the offices of The QT Talent Agency Amanda has not returned my calls once, therefore we don't keep missing each other. I keep missing her and she keeps ignoring me!'

But I didn't.

Later that evening I received an email from a Don Block. Acting assistant manager at The QT Talent Agency.

Ver-fucking-batim.

'Given the recent tragic events at The QT Talent agency we are re-evaluating all the work that our irreplaceable and much missed boss Quentin Talisman had green-lit including *The Irrelevant Playthings of a Cosmic Giant*. Sadly, the new reader that has been assigned to 'Playthings' does not feel as enthused about the work as Quentin, and I unfortunately must concur. With the understandable current upheaval at the agency we are striving to ensure that only writers and novels taken on up to late last year will be represented as planned. I know this is very disappointing news for you but there are probably loads of agents out there who feel differently. Still I cannot commit to a work unless I truly believe in it so belatedly we at QT will have to reverse the decision and pass on the project.'

And that, ladies and gentlemen, is my contribution to this public platform for creative misfortune, poetic futility and lost artistic dreams.

THE STORY FROM THE CHARLIE AND THE CONTENDERS CHAPBOOK

MOTHER'S DAY

Mother is in hospital. She isn't very well. She is eighty-two years old. She has recently been diagnosed with vascular dementia. The medical term is vascular. They leave out the next word. Dementia. They are discreet like that. Understated. Play things down. Like being diagnosed with lung cancer and told you are suffering from lung.

She was sitting up in bed yesterday. The shell-shocked look of the old. A vacant vessel in a cotton nightie. I noticed her ancient fretting hands. Those grisly guests, seen in close-up, on every television report about elder care. Conversation was minimal.

'What are you doing?'

'Having a think.'

'About what?'

'Nothing.'

She is sleeping now. Already looks blue dead. Sunken cheeks. Thin lips. I feel terrorized. I shouldn't be. I should be rational. And remember when I was a child. And watched an old black and white movie. And an elderly character died. What did I think? I thought old things die.

It's the most natural thing in the world. Or recall when I was twelve. Grandad died. What did I think? Old things die. It's the most natural thing in the world. Or Trouble, my beloved Jack Russell. Must have been one-hundred-and-ten in dog years, when he collapsed that night in the kitchen. Old things die. It's the most natural thing in the world. But now it's mother. And what do I think? I think please God – and to paraphrase Nick Cave, I don't even believe in an interventionist you – please make her better. Don't take her now. Some other time.

When will that consultant Dr Murphy turn up? Consultants seem to operate in a sort of Bermuda triangle in hospitals. And yet they get paid so much. Imagine getting all that money for being a glorified disappearing act. I find an overworked nurse. Says she'll be there in a minute.

I return to the room. It's Mother's Day. Irony of ironies. I finger the card I've brought. Don't think she'll be reading that today. Not a particularly good card anyway. Amber flowers. Kitsch silver writing. I wonder how many mothers pass away on Mother's Day.

Lost in memory. Two flashbacks. Waiting for mother to go to bed. Part one. April 1973. Around nine-thirty in the evening. Father is away. Mother is reading the newspaper on the kitchen table, tells me to go to bed now but that she'll be up soon to kiss me goodnight. I go upstairs. Wash my teeth. Put on my pyjamas. Say my prayers. Interventionist God. Big in my life in those days. Hit the sack. Lie awake. She forgets to come up. I wait and wait. Am possessed by a self-pitying frenzy. I can't sleep. I get upset. What is she doing? She said she'd be up in a minute. How long does it take to read a newspaper? How could she forget to kiss her son goodnight? She doesn't really love me. That's it. I'm the middle child. Always ignored. The oldest is special. It's the first child. The youngest is special. It's the baby of the house. The middle? The middle is the middle. Two hours go by. I finally hear her on the upstairs landing.

'You said you'd come up and say goodnight to me, mammy,' I whisper loudly trying not to wake my younger brother, Gerry. She comes in. I repeat my sentence, deflated and injured. 'Sorry dear, I forgot.' She kisses me on the forehead goodnight.

Waiting for mother to go to bed. Part two. February 2012. Back home on a visit. It is ten past eleven at night. I lie awake in bed. She is still downstairs. Pottering about. She said she'd be up in a minute. A quarter-of-an-hour ago. What is she doing? Turning off the lights? Getting a glass of water? Turning on the oven? I fret.

I can't sleep. I finally get up. I open my bedroom door. She is making her way up the stairs. In slow motion. All Gollum wizened. I admonish her. 'You said you'd come up ages ago.' 'Sorry dear, I forgot.' I kiss her on the forehead goodnight.

She started to decline about two years ago. She had intermittent vertigo so they decided she should go to falling classes. It basically entailed her going to this place every Wednesday morning at eleven o'clock and, for an hour, with a group of other elderly ladies she learned to fall properly. Then one day she fell. And didn't get up. The funny thing is, at the same time I was going to standing classes. I had gone to a Tai-Chi instructor on Wicklow Street. He told me about these standing classes he ran separately for his pupils, who, if they were too busy (or in my case lazy) to practice the movements he had taught them in their weekly Tai-Chi class, could always come to his studio another time during the week and pay him twenty euro for him to oversee them semi-squat and stand for an hour. So there was mother doing falling classes, and I was heading off to do standing classes. A beautiful and absurd connection between a mother and her son.

The nurse has just looked in. Assures me mother's breathing is normal and not the dreaded 'death rattle'. She closes the curtain to keep out the afternoon sun. She points at mother.

'She's a right Lee Marvin, that one.'

'What do you mean?'

'A wandering star.'

I nod.

'Found her up on the second floor last night.'

Gerry and Kieran have rung from Australia. I stare at mother again. She looks just like one of her brothers, my uncle Derek when he was dying. Or had died. She is a corpse-in-waiting.

The past is like Hotel California. You can check out anytime you want but you can never leave. It is a mischievous stalker. It keeps coming up behind you and kicking you in the pants. And everything comes full circle. Your mother collects you after your first day at school. You collect her after her first day in the day care centre. You ask her what it was like. Awful. Full of old people.

What goes 'round comes 'round. She berates you when you are a teenager. Sitting in a darkened room. Hiding from life.

'Will you get out from under my feet. You've me driven daft. Look at your friend Eddie Hourican down the road, off working in that summer job every morning. Or your cousins Joe and Mick working on the trains, and what are doing with yourself? Sitting and staring!'

Years later. Same story. Roles reversed. I enter the same darkened room. Thirty summers may have come and gone but those venetian blinds and that carpet – design: psychedelic vomit – remain the same. I become exasperated at her resigned benign lethargy.

'Look at Eddie Hourican's parents, down the road, still walking every day, fit as fiddles, Theo still swims and Maureen still plays the odd round of golf. Look at your older brother Raymond. Eighty-eight in July. On a treadmill each morning. A treadmill! And look at you. Just sitting and staring.'

Mother died half-an-hour ago. Thanks for nothing

interventionist God. They've opened the window to let her spirit out. That's what they do around these parts. Still no sign of Dr Murphy. I dump the card in the bin. And kiss her on the forehead goodnight.

AT HOME WITH RACHEL

'Lovely red wine, Rachel. Saint-Emilion will never let you down.'

'Is it finished?'

'Unfortunately.'

'Oh well. One more for the bottle bank.'

'I cherish my trips to the bottle bank.'

'I know.'

'No small talk. If there is one place a complete stranger will never strike up a conversation with you it is at the bottle bank.'

'Karl, you should put that in your book.'

'Maybe.'

'Do.'

'You've got this strange grin on your face, Rachel. What are you smiling at?'

'I hope you don't mind, but I've read some of your stories.'

'What?!'

'I was going through a few things. They were lying on the desk.'

'Rachel, I never gave you permission to look at the stories.'

'Come off it, darling. I was curious, that's all. And

you were so disappointed no one has taken the time to look at them. '

'But you had no right.'

'What do you mean? We live together. We share a life. Just wanted to know what you were working on. And I'm a good reader. Have been doing it since I was six.'

'That's not the point. It's just...'

'What? Are you saying that I'm incapable of having a constructive opinion? Oh, it's only old Rachel. Is that it? I studied English at UCD.'

'Yeh, for only six months, before you took that job in the bank.'

'I know what this is about. You're still sore. Over your most recent unpublished novel. That was over four years ago. You asked me to be brutally frank.'

'There is brutally frank and sadistically frank.'

'That's not fair!'

'Really? Pretentious. Solipsistic.'

'It was an honest assessment.'

'Trite. Will I go on?'

'I thought I was helping.'

'Helping? I happen to believe that *Bonjour Disappointment* is the best thing I have ever written! And it is a travesty, an absolute travesty that it never found a publisher!'

'Ok, I'll never look at anything you write ever again. Happy?'

'Ah, for fuck sake, don't be like that. Stop over-reacting.'

'*I'm* over-reacting?'

'No, no wait. Rachel, wait. Maybe I did get a bit overexcited. Wait, I'm sorry.'

'Hmmm.'

'So, uh, uhm, eh... what did you think of them?'

'No, it's ok, it's ok, I'm not going to tell you now. I'm not in the mood.'

'Ah, come on.'

'No. No. The moment has passed.'

'Well, did you think they were any good?'

'I'm not saying.'

'Ah for Jesus sake.'

'No.'

'Well, if that's the way you want it. Great! Little Miss Sulky drawers! Ruining another evening with your moods.'

'*My* moods? Oh, fuck off. I'm going to bed.'

'Nighty night then.'

'Nighty night. Oh by the way, for you, tonight, it'll be Bonjour Sofa!'

THREE OF THE STORIES RACHEL PERUSED

GALWAY'S GREATEST LOVER

When I walked into Galway city as a young adult in the 1980s, I always passed this man in Lower Salthill who would be leaning over a low gate with his belly hanging out. And I would ask myself 'Who is this man leaning over a low gate with his belly hanging out?'

One day, many years later, I was looking out my upstairs window, and I leant over and my belly popped out. And at that very moment I thought of the man. The man leaning over the low gate with his belly hanging out. And I realized, I was now that man. This is what I, Ambrose Aloysius Thornton, had become. Just a man. Looking out. Watching the world go by. With my belly hanging out.

I decided I needed to change. I didn't want to be just another anonymous fat man looking out an upstairs window. I didn't want to turn into Robert Mitchum, who had once said, 'People think I have an interesting walk, hell, I'm just trying to hold my gut in.' I didn't want to become girth-bogglingly obese with all that accumulated visceral fat leading to a possible premature expiry date. I had to get rid of my papoose of pudge. Naked, I had started to look like one of those unfortunates in a Lucien Freud painting. I had to get into shape. A friend suggested I could do with a bit of colonic irrigation. Not overtly enthused with the idea initially, another friend then suggested it could be a 'good way of meeting women.' I have pretty strange friends.

And that's how I came to meet Janine.

I first asked Janine out at her place of work in Healthy Matter, a colonic hydrotherapy clinic on Fr Griffin Road.

She had just stuck her surgical-gloved finger up my rectum and told me my prostate was fine. She was now proceeding to gently flood my colon with some warm water via a delicately placed tube up my anus to help banish all residual toxins and faecal materials – the impacted waste as they call it on their brochure – when the 'good way of meeting women' idea re-surfaced in my mind. If ever there was a correct time to ask a woman out, I felt, this was it. If she said no it wouldn't be a source of disappointment. I had already been utterly humiliated and degraded in her company. And she did seem so nice. Sweetly supportive as I felt that over-powering feeling of fullness in my stomach and started evacuating a particularly gushing bowel movement.

I turned my head towards her.

'A new restaurant is opening on Abbeygate Street. This might not seem the correct time to discuss food, or possible romance, but I have two complimentary tickets for the launch of The Hunger Strike – a post-modern slightly offensive name, you may agree – on Thursday night, would you like to accompany me?'

She paused. I evacuated some more.

'I don't usually date clients.'

With the aplomb of an artist, Janine then removed the tube and wiped me clean. I sought clarity.

'So that's a no, then.'

Janine nodded.

I persisted. During the spring I had four more colonic cleansing sessions. Each time I went to Healthy Matter I asked Janine for a date. Finally, she acquiesced. She agreed to meet me. The Event: Local sculptor Manfred Mullarkey's quietly humorous peat figurines of some well-known national characters. The Time: 6.30 p.m. Friday the 12th. The Location: The Galway Arts Centre, Dominick Street. It was my first date in three years. What could I bring her as a gift?

I remembered reading quite a positive review of a book in the *New York Times* best-seller list a few years back by Syracuse-based Dr Nathan Bandello called *The Turd Man – Memoirs of a Colonic Hydrotherapist*.

The book chronicled Nathan's passion for his particular occupation after both his parents had died of colon cancer before he was twenty and how he vowed to make colonic irrigation his life's work to help prevent the onset of this potentially fatal disease in as many people as possible. He did this because he did not want to have other families experience what he and his younger sister Amy, now a successful media lawyer in San Diego, had gone through. Tragically, after the book's outstanding success Nathan had unfortunately succumbed to colon cancer himself. Like that jogging guy who wrote that jogging book years ago and then dropped dead jogging. I was determined to buy an earlier edition of the book so Janine would not find out about Nathan's untimely demise in the updated blurb.

That is if I decided to actually go ahead and buy her the book. Would Janine *really* be interested in this book? Surely, given her line of work she'd like a bit of escapism and adventure rather than a forensic analysis of the workings of the large intestine. Possibly it was the last thing she wanted to read. Anyway, maybe she had the book already. Given to her as a Christmas present or birthday present one year. Then again, colonic hydrotherapy had brought us together, in a roundabout way, so maybe she would find my gesture deeply romantic. I concluded to have a look at the book first and make a decision about purchasing on the spur of the moment.

Two days before our rendezvous, I went to Eason's bookshop on Shop Street. No sign of the book on the shelves. I approached the counter.

'Do you have a book called *The Turd Man – Memoirs of a Colonic Hydrotherapist* by a Dr Nathan Bandello? It was a big hit in the States a few years back.'

The name tag said Bernard. He looked like a pillow in a condom. He blinked behind the cash register and stared at me.

'The one with Orson Welles, is it? We don't do DVDs here. Go across the road to Zhivago Music.'

I decided I was going to buy Janine flowers instead.

But I had a more pressing problem. Over the years, I had realized that if premature ejaculation were an Olympic sport I'd be a gold medalist. The four-second man. How come I'm always good at stuff that never gets recognized?

Now, there were other reasons my ex-wife Cliona had left me in late 2011 for that Californian, new-age, ski-pants wearing reflexologist, Chad Webb, and Cliona had made that quite clear.

'It's not *that*. It's all the other stuff. *As well*.'

'What other stuff?'

'The not talking. The sighing. The pacing. The drinking. The griping. About the country. About your work. About the weather. The not turning up when you are supposed to. The turning up when you are not supposed to. The not listening to me when I talk. The snoring. The storming out and not having an argument when we are all set to have an argument. The need to be praised when you wash the dishes *once* in six months. The need to be praised when you cook a meal *once* in six years and the never ever *ever* wanting to go out.'

Cliona was right. I had never liked going out. But that's just the way I am. All my life I was surrounded by people who went out in the evening and did things while

I stayed in. My parents, Noel and Eucharia Thornton, were people who liked to go out in the evening and do things while I stayed in. Later, in the few flats I lived in, my flat-mates were always interested in going out in the evening and doing things while I stayed in. Then I met Cliona. She liked going out in the evening and doing things while I stayed in. But what is so *wrong* with staying in?

My biggest thrill in life was to be invited to a dinner party, accept the invitation reluctantly, only at the last minute for the hostess to cancel. There was no greater joy in my life than a surprise night *in*!

But that was Cliona and the past is Sri Lanka as that writer said. Or a foreign country. Or something like that. And now it was time to focus on Janine. What happens if Janine and myself end up in bed after our first date? I decided, just in case the situation arose, so to speak, to undertake some online research to curb my, ahem, timing issue. There were two techniques constantly referred to, to help alleviate my problem with overhasty seed delivery. The stop/start technique. And the stop/squeeze technique. They both basically entailed prolonged bouts of masturbation with delay of orgasm for as long as possible. Since becoming a victim of downsizing and company re-structuring and losing my job as chief marketing manager at Sofa So Good on the Limerick road, spare time was something I had an abundance of and I embraced these exercises with a rare enthusiasm. After an intensive 18-hour work-out, I had shown small signs of improvement by managing 35 seconds from erection to ejaculation with the stop/start exercise and 41 seconds from erection to ejaculation with the stop/squeeze exercise. Not bad. But *could do better.*

I wanted to have all the angles covered. The conversation side of the evening, for example. How could I ensure that went well? Just before heading out to meet her, I undertook some last minute planning by consulting some websites on tips for dating. One website claimed that if you go on a date and you agree with everything your date says, she will not be impressed. If you disagree with everything she says, she will not be impressed either.

However if you disagree with her on the first half of the date and then gradually start to agree with her over the second half, then she will start to like you, and this is the *coup de grace,* the later you delay the change from disagreeing to agreeing, the more successful you will be.

While mulling over possible topics to initially disagree about before gradually changing my mind... a holistic approach to healthcare, a need for improved street lighting in Lower Salthill, the origin of the word polyp, old French or Latin?, peat as a raw material for creative endeavor... I received a text. It was from Janine. Something unexpected had come up and she had to cancel at the last minute.

Oh joy of joys! Another surprise night in.

ZIGGY STARDUST RUINED MY LIFE

Monday the 11th of January 2016. David Bowie is dead. The world is in mourning. Except for one person.

60-year-old Irish woman, Molly Moynihan.

'It's because of that man I'm an old maid. It's because of that man I've been left on the shelf. It's because of that man I have no eyebrows.'

Molly remembers July 1972 vividly. Sixteen-years-old, watching television with her parents, Bernard and Assumpta.

'We lived in Wicklow. Which meant we had the English TV channels. Most of the rest of the country didn't. That's when I saw him. Like something from another galaxy singing 'Starman' on Top of The Pops. Ziggy Stardust changed my life. But not in a good way.'

Obsessed with Ziggy, Molly, up until then a cautious and pragmatic girl, took the early bus to Bray, one Saturday the following month, and entering Clodagh's Hair Salon requested to have her eyebrows plucked. On her return home, her father was in such a state of shock he placed his newly lit pipe in the goldfish bowl (sadly Goldie did not survive) while her mother immediately fell to her knees and started strangling a pair of rosary beads.

'Mammy and Daddy were very put out. Over the next few months, any time the relatives turned up, mammy got me to tell everybody I had a rare blood disorder. If I remember correctly, we decided to call it Rudimeister's Syndrome.'

Then in February 1973. Disaster.

'Some of the girls found out about it in school. David had done this big gig in Hammersmith, London and announced he was killing off Ziggy. We couldn't believe it. It was such a selfish thing to do. But over the years he was always a bit like that. It was always about him, wasn't it? I want to follow my artistic journey. I want to be a major cultural figure and constantly evolve. I'm going to be a shape changer – whatever the hell that means! But what about the fans? And what about all those shaved off eyebrows!'

Molly claims there were seven other eyebrow-less girls in her class that year. Only two found husbands in the interim.

'Emer Nesbitt met a guard from Newbridge and June Kilbride married one of the Fureys from Gorey.'

By 1975 David Bowie had found American soul, and Molly had found Leo Sayer.

'Leo was much more 'me' really. Don't know what I ever saw in David, frankly.'

But sadly, as the years progressed the disappearance and subsequent non re-appearance of her eyebrows became an ongoing issue with prospective male suitors.

'As I got older, I tried everything. I attempted to recreate the pencil-thin Marlene Dietrich look but I'm built like a combine harvester and I've got that ruddy-cheeked farmer's wife look from my father's people in Castlerea, so Weimar Republic elegance and my genetic palette were not exactly a match made in heaven.'

Alternative remedies were also considered and dismissed.

'I had to put my foot down when that Chinese acupuncturist in Waterford mentioned badger semen. I said no, no, Lin-Lin I am not going there, I am sorry but there are certain limits to what I'll try. '

She even travelled abroad to try and find a solution.

'I spent an absolute fortune flying to Zurich to Dr Hans Pfifferlinger's world-renowned Follicular Unit Transplantation Clinic. Did it get my eyebrows back? Yes. One snag though. I ended up looking like a close personal relative of Leonid Brezhnev. The procedure had to be reversed.'

In reality, it was extremely difficult for Molly to find a man who was attracted to a woman with no eyebrows. And if one did turn up he was usually very odd. And there were few men odder than Theodore J. Cuddihy.

Theodore J. Cuddihy, scion of the famous Cuddihy family and estate in Baltinglass, wore jodhpurs under his pyjamas, was fluent in Finnish and had a slightly unnatural obsession with the actor Harry Dean Stanton. He was also ommatrichophobic. Ommatrichophobia is a person who has a phobia about eyebrows.

'To be completely honest, Theodore fell down a bit on the wooing and romancing side of things,' Molly recalls.

'He approached our nascent relationship like a business arrangement. He even sent his valet, Dixon, around to propose marriage on his behalf. One morning Dixon turns up at our house and reads out a note in Theodore's handwriting. Molly you are not really my ideal woman, it stated, but because of my phobia I have an extremely small number of women, apart from some of your ex-classmates, to choose from in the greater Wicklow, Wexford and Carlow area. I am basically looking for a wife, companion and reproductive vessel for my future children. Any thoughts on the matter?'

Molly sighs at the memory.

'Mammy who was also in the room looked over at me and said, I know what you're thinking but you can't deny that he's a good catch.'

After some dithering Molly accepted the proposal and promptly kissed a stunned Dixon on the lips. However, the marriage was never to take place, as unbeknownst to Molly, Theodore, to increase his chances of an heir, had also commenced an association with June Kilbride who had walked out on the Furey from Gorey and was to become Mrs. Theodore J. Cuddihy the following spring.

How can one man have wreaked such havoc?

Not Cuddihy.

Bowie.

Molly sums up the whole sorry affair.

'He was the man who fell to earth. He was the man who sold the world. He was the man who ruined my life.'

WHENEVER

Someone comes to the house last month. He rings the bell. Is he one of those guys who wants to clear the gutter on the roof? They turn up around this time of year. I open the door. No, he's too well dressed. I tell him whatever he is selling I am not interested. If he wants to sell me some energy deal or some broadband special offer. Not interested. He informs me it's nothing to do with that. It's another matter, entirely. Like what? I inquire. He looks away for a moment. He then asks me did I ever hear of the grim reaper? I said sure, everyone has heard of the grim... There is a long pause. I try to remain calm. I look at the guy. I say, you? He nods. Wait a minute, I'm only thirty-eight-years old. I've got my whole life in front of me. No you don't. Not anymore, he says. He tells me he is sorry. He says he tells everyone that. He is very apologetic. I begin to well up. He offers me a handkerchief. Always has one handy, he says. Go on cry, he says. It's good to cry. Let it all out. Not enough men have cried over the centuries. That's one of the things that's wrong with the world. A philosopher too, I ponder, as I wipe away my tears.

I start to reflect. If I'd had an interesting life, this would have been the moment it would have flashed in front of me. But nothing flashes in front of me. My mind is blank. Other people's interesting lives start popping into my head. People whose obituaries I've read over the last few years. T.K. Whitaker – an Irish patriot in the truest sense of the word. Chancellor of the National University of Ireland, President of The Royal Irish Academy, esteemed civil servant and senator, who in his spare time single-handedly saved Ireland from financial ruin in the late 1950s. Actor John Hurt – Golden Globe winner, BAFTA award winner, CBE, Knighthood and on top of that copious drinking, incessant smoking, four wives and countless lovers! Maya Angelou – talk about overcoming the odds! From humble dysfunctional upbringing in a racist world to receiving fifty honorary degrees and writing seven autobiographies! How can anybody receive fifty honorary degrees and write seven autobiographies, in whatever lifespan you are allotted? These people led phenomenal lives. Obituaries are published just to make the rest of us mere mortals (and here's one mere who won't be mortal much longer) feel like worthless exponents of non-achievement. What did *I* ever do?

Swiftly coming to terms with my acute sense of unremarkable, I decide if this is to be my final day, so be it. There is an awkward silence. To help fill it, my front door visitor starts to go into more detail about his job. He's using a sat nav now, but he still gets lost sometimes. He runs up a lot of travel expenses and trying to claim them back at the end of the year is always a drag. He hates dogs in a driveway. I realize he's 'grim' in the joyless sense of the word as opposed to the ghastly sense of the word. He should be called the grumbling reaper or the griping reaper. But I quite like his curmudgeonly candid manner. In fact, I start to positively warm to this chap. We're cut from the same cloth and I won't mind spending time with him. Whatever *that* entails. He works through a further list of complaints. He tells me he's getting old. He doesn't want to do this anymore. He was never a good traveler. He's got a weak stomach. He'd love to just pack it in and take it easy. Put his feet up. Smoke his pipe. One of the last pipe smokers left. Go fishing. But you know what? Someone has to do his job, right? Overpopulation the way it is, it's getting crazy. I concur. Wholeheartedly. I ask him, so how do we go about this death thing? Do I need to pack anything? Pyjamas? Toothbrush? Bite guard? Non-stick saucepan? He points to a black Range Rover across the street. No. I just have to follow him and get in the back of the range rover, he says, everything will be taken care of and then he'll tick my name, Ronan McCarthy, off the list. He puts on a pair of glasses and shows me my name on the list to prove everything is above board. I peer down at the name. I look again. I start to smirk. I shake my head and sigh. I've resigned myself to this big adventure but suddenly disappointment has barged in once again, like a drunken stag party interrupting an early morning stakeout of birdwatchers. Wrong guy, I tell him. My name *is* Ronan MacCarthy, I explain, but I spell my surname 'mac'. What do you mean? he asks. I tell him that's the story of my life. Maybe it's the only story. That one thing. Throughout all those years the amount of people who get the spelling of my surname wrong. The amount of misdirected emails I've received at work. Utility companies sending out bills with the incorrect spelling. It's a minefield. People don't think it matters, 'mc', 'mac'. It *does* matter. How one spells one's surname matters! He becomes slightly agitated. He apologizes once more. He begins another reticent rant. He thinks the standards at work have plummeted since they put everything on that computer system. Nowadays, there are endless glitches and mix-ups. In the old days, when they used a good old-fashioned paper trail, there were far fewer mistakes. If it ain't broke, why fix it? But no. Technology demanded a complete overhaul. He wheezes slightly. Then he tells me there's talk of privatization next year, even out-sourcing, with more and more companies entering the market. The all-round quality of service will decline. Logistically, he says, it'll be a complete nightmare. He removes an iPad from a leather folder. I hate these things, he tells me. He scrolls down a bit. I'm going to have to look into this, he announces. There's probably been a mistake. Finland is the worst for spelling mishaps he says, followed by Hungary. And don't get him started on Indonesia. He smiles weakly. There is a pause. Nice meeting you, Ronan. We'll see each other again, sometime. He nods. I shrug my shoulders. Whenever.

THE KARL MACDERMOTT ARCHIVE PART TWO

THE FIVE COMPLETED BLOG ENTRIES FROM *A MOAN AGAIN, NATURALLY* – 2013

SOUNDTRACK OF OUR TIMES – January 1st, 2013

I am writing this while listening to a neighbour's house alarm ring incessantly. The clangorous house alarm in the near distance. A soundtrack of our times. Why do people need house alarms? Simple. Because some people have things and other people have less things. And the people with less things want the things the people with things have. And the people with things don't want the people with less things to get their things so they get an alarm. Which goes off a lot of the time when the people with less things aren't even trying to get the things the people with things have. Because of dodgy wiring. Or the wind. Or birds on the roof. But whatever sets the alarm off – we the rest of the population, which includes people with other things and people with absolutely no things – have to listen to the alarm. Excuse me now, while I locate and put on an old pair of spectacles I have. Of the rose-tinted variety. When I was growing up, we literally *did* leave the back door open all day. No one had alarms. Why was that? Because we *all* had things? Or no one wanted the things we had. My father's James Last records spring to mind. Or maybe the things we had were too cumbersome to rob. TVs were the size of enormous cookers in those days. Or maybe it was because we never had the *latest* things. Nobody bought the *latest* things. Or if we did buy an up-to-date model, by the time we'd saved up to finally complete the transaction the product would be already, technologically, two years out-of-date on day of delivery. And then it would be held on to until it 'sat down'. People's things lasted. TV's and stereo systems were replaced every nine to fourteen years. Will now remove old pair of spectacles and try to find those earplugs that were purchased in Cadiz over a decade ago.

HELL IS OTHER PEOPLE (AT THE CINEMA) – January 2nd, 2013

Know what I hate? Coffee-to-go stragglers at the cinema. Today I encountered one again. As always, I arrived early for a screening. I found my favourite seat. I dutifully sat through the puerile ads. I watched all types of people enter. The solitary cinema-goer who looks like a nun on holidays. The group of giddy students and their amplified banter. And the couples. If it is early in the relationship they instantly agree with one another where to sit, if it is somewhat later in the relationship where to sit can become a source of much debate, eyes to heaven and sighing. I re-watched the trailers I've already seen countless times and settled back waiting for the movie to start. As the houselights were about to be dimmed I felt safe. I did not have any proximity issue with my fellow cinemagoer, at best the cinema was half-full, and I had plenty of leg room. On both sides. But just as the opening credits appeared I noticed a shaft of light as the cinema door opened. Suddenly, I was convulsed with tension. I then saw one. The coffee-to-go straggler! The coffee-to-go straggler held his cardboard cup of coffee and planet ruining plastic lid with one hand and with the other used his smartphone as torch. I watched him warily as he peered around deciding where he wanted to sit. As the opening credits came to an end, he was still shuffling around but then of course, eureka! He had spotted an empty seat. I am not using overstatement here. My world completely collapsed. I knew where he had decided to sit. Yes, he was approaching, a fait accompli for the gods, laughing now as usual, and in no time he looked down at me and asked, 'Can I sit here?' 'Sure.' I moved my stuff. And then he had the temerity to use my cinema seat cup holder for his cup of coffee. 'I'm sorry, but that's my cup holder. Yours is the other side.' I declared curtly. 'But you're not using it.' 'I use it for my elbow.' To maintain pretense, I spent the rest of the movie with my elbow lodged in the cup holder of my seat. Not to be recommended. I think I've developed carpal tunnel syndrome.

ZOO STORY – January 3rd, 2013

I went to the zoo recently. There was some special deal. After twenty minutes I found myself standing outside the hut of the red speckled Borneo dwarf hippo. And he wouldn't come out. And I waited. Still, he wouldn't come out. But I continued to wait. Because I'd paid my money and I was determined to see that goddamned red speckled Borneo dwarf hippo. At this particular moment in my life, I happened to be passing by his hut, I wouldn't be backtracking to see him in an hour when I'd be in a different part of the zoo looking at the rhinos and the antelopes, but did that red speckled Borneo dwarf hippo come out of his hut? No. Then I remembered the last time I was at the zoo about thirty years ago. The exact same thing happened. That time I was with my parents and I think it may have been the rare three-eared proboscis freak monkey from Equatorial New Guinea that proved particularly shy and withdrawn. Back then our whole family waited half-an-hour and not one of those three-eared freak monkeys came out from their hut. It bothered me back then and it bothers me now. The fact that sometimes the animal refuses to come out. You pay good money and you don't get to see them. I feel like writing a letter of complaint to David Attenborough!

PERSISTENT POLISH BARMAIDS–January 4th, 2013

I ordered a pint of Guinness on Friday in O'Neill's on Suffolk Street at about ten past five. It hadn't yet filled up with the post-work office crowd, I had an hour to kill and I saw a spare table in one of the snugs. So I sat and waited for the barmaid to pull my pint. And I waited. And waited. And I took out my newspaper (the last of the luddites) and tried to read it. But the lighting was too dark. I couldn't relax. I looked around and I saw an old fat man grunting loudly at the bar. I saw two women talking and texting at the table next to me. I moved around in my sunken green seat uncomfortably, one of those seats turned yellow and soft from overuse. I resumed my attempt to read the paper. But, still, I couldn't relax. Suddenly I realized I don't want to be here for the next hour. Maybe I should cut back on my drinking anyway – New Year resolutions and all that. So I quickly packed away my newspaper, grabbed my coat and ran out the door. I crossed the street hurriedly like some furtive burglar, looking behind me as if the barmaid was going to come chasing after me with the freshly pulled pint. I stopped at a shop window trying to immerse myself in the passing crowd. I looked back once again and to my horror the barmaid *had* actually come out of the pub with the freshly pulled pint. She spotted me and ran across the street trying not to spill the pint. I ran inside a sportswear shop but she followed me in. Cornering me near the changing room area she said 'Here. That'll be €4.80 please.' I knew it. She didn't look Irish. And she had an East European accent. One of those persistent Polish barmaids! I fumbled embarrassedly for the right amount but only had five euro. I gave it to her. I was debating whether to leave her a tip when she handed over the change. She promptly turned around and left. I held onto my pint, looked around and sneaked into the changing room and sat down. I started sipping my pint. Not surprisingly, I was still failing to feel relaxed. Suddenly, the curtain was pulled back. 'You can't drink that here,' the shop assistant said, as a customer waited impatiently to try on a ski suit. I left the shop and walked across the street holding my pint. I loitered momentarily outside a bubble tea and juice bar restaurant but saw two Gardaí at the bottom of the street approaching. I walked up the road and, finally, accepting my fate, went back into O'Neill's of Suffolk Street. The barmaid was bringing an order to another table and when she saw me she just shook her head and sighed. The pub had filled up by this stage and my seat had been taken. I stood next to the crowded bar and while trying to awkwardly finish my pint, a tall gentleman spilt a glass of crème de menthe on my just-back-from-the-dry-cleaners cream chinos.

THE PEOPLE WHO REALLY KILLED KENNEDY – November 22nd, 2013

John F. Kennedy is dead fifty years today. I have this theory about who was behind his assassination. And it is so blindingly obvious, I am amazed no one else has propounded the idea. Anti-Castro Cubans? No. The CIA? No. The Mafia? No. Lee Harvey Oswald? No. Hat manufacturers. John F. Kennedy single-handedly destroyed the hat wearing industry in the United States and worldwide in the early 1960s. Before Kennedy was elected president, most men in the western world wore hats. After Kennedy entered the White House, because he had become an unlikely fashion icon and didn't wear a hat, men around the world stopped wearing hats. My supposition is, by mid-1963, the global kingpins of the hat manufacturing industry finally realized how toxic Kennedy was to their sales and decided they had to do something about it. They figured, after the event, things would go back to the way they were. After all, Lyndon B. Johnson wore a hat. But they forgot one thing. Who in their right mind wanted to look like Lyndon B. Johnson?

KARL VISITS HIS PSYCHOANALYST

'So, Karl, how are you this weather?'

'Churchill had his black dog. I've got my melan-collie.'

'Feeling a bit down are we?'

'Comes and goes, Dr Kinsella.'

'How's the writing going?'

'Actually, I'm working on a book of short fiction at the moment.'

'Really? Well, if it ever gets published let me know. I'll pick up a copy somewhere. My wife Carmel is a big reader.'

'Uh-huh.'

'Or, maybe email me a few of the stories. It could help with this whole process and your specific case.'

'Ok.'

'I don't envy you. Must be a hard old graft, the old writing.'

'Yeh.'

'Still you're doing what you want.'

'Yeh.'

'Not much money in it?'

'No.'

'As long as you're happy.'

'Hmmm.'

'Of course. If you were happy you wouldn't be here.'

'Guess I wouldn't.'

'Well, I know I've mentioned this before but there are three principles behind Cognitive Behavioral Therapy. Firstly, how we choose to view the world can influence our mood. Secondly, our mood and our thoughts are linked. Thirdly, learning that we can influence our thoughts can therefore greatly improve our mood. So let's just try a little exercise in word association. I say a word and you say the first thing that comes into your head. Ready?'

'Yeh.'

'Tipperary.'

'A long way.'

'Cork.'

'Clannish.'

'Kerry.'

'Cute Hoors.'

'Mayo.'

'The Blessed Virgin Mary.'

'Sligo.'

'Yeats. Snobs.'

'Galway.'

'Over-rated. Over-priced. Wet.'

'Clare.'

'Diddle. Dee. Fuckin. Eye.'

'Limerick.'

'Samurai Skangers.'
'Laois.'
'Belgium.'
'Cavan.'
'Sheep fuckers.'
'Monaghan.'
'More sheep fuckers.'
'Meath.'
'Just Fuckers.'
'Donegal.'
'Cúpla fuckers.'
'Louth.'
'Semtex.'
'Carlow.'
'Next.'
'Wicklow.'
'Garden.'
'Dublin.'
'So-called wit.'
'Kildare.'
'Horses.'
'Roscommon.'
'Uh...'
'Waterford.'
'Child abuse.'
'Wexford.'
'In-breeding.'
'Kilkenny.'

'Home to the world famous 'city' of the same name.'

'Longford.'

'Hairpieces.'

'Westmeath.'

'Death.'

'Offaly.'

'Go away.'

'Leitrim.'

'Lovely.'

'Right, that was an interesting experiment and I think what it highlights is you are feeling a certain anger, and of course depression is anger directed inwards, so there is a strong correlation between the two, but also you feel a certain disconnect with your Irishness and Ireland. Would I be correct in this analysis?'

'Possibly.'

'Did you ever hear of Abraham Maslow?'

'I think I read about him somewhere.'

'Well, in 1943 he came up with a theory about human beings' hierarchy of needs. In order to be able to function, a human being requires these five needs to be satisfied. We can go into the others again but a sense of belonging is one of them. Feeling part of a community. I don't think you feel you belong. I don't think you feel part of a community.'

'Well to paraphrase Groucho Marx, I wouldn't want to be part of a community that would have me as a member of that community.'

'I see, but scientific research states that the older you become the more important it is to feel that sense of belonging, a sense of place.'

'My only sense of place is in my head.'

'Wisecracks are all very well, and if that's who you feel you are then that is perfectly fine. Our approach to everything should be a non-judgmental one and if you are happy to be set apart from your community that is your prerogative. And of course, the corollary of a non-judgmental position is acceptance. Self-acceptance. 'To thine own self be true,' that famous line from *Hamlet*. How do you feel about your ability to accept yourself?'

'I'm not great on that. I'd rate my self-acceptance at ★★ at the very most. And I'm using a ★★★★★ system.'

'The self-criticism is very revealing, Karl. But it's not an intractable situation. You see, eh, we all have choices in life. Every minute in every day we can make a decision to change.'

'But wait a minute, on the one hand you say accept yourself but now on the other hand you've just said you can change. Isn't that a bit of a contradiction?'

'Ehm. Uh... let me see... on the contrary. There are no definite answers to anything, there are only questions, and debating the questions helps us arrive at possible solutions, but the important thing is to examine all the options in our psychoanalytical journey of discovery. No one said it would be a quick journey. Sometimes it can be a lifetime of exploration.'

'A lifetime? Thank God for the public health system.'

'Yes. Quite. I think we've made steady progress today, Karl and have had a very productive half-hour. You can arrange another appointment with Evelyn at the desk for some time next month. Alright?'

'Thank you, Dr Kinsella. So, I'll email you a few of the stories?'

'Sorry?'

'The stories. You said email me a few of the stories.'

'Oh, yes. Of course. Yes. The stories. Evelyn will give you my email address.'

THREE STORIES THAT SIT INDEFINITELY IN DOCTOR KINSELLA'S INBOX

THE MALACHY MISSION

Every time I met Malachy Mulrooney, he had a cold. On the street always sneezing. Endless coughing and spluttering while waiting for the elevator. In a coffee shop, I sometimes saw him use empty sugar sachets to clean his nose because he'd run out of tissue. On the disgusting human behaviour Richter scale, that's a seven. I was tired of all this, I mean we worked in the same building, shared the same canteen, stood (and exhaled) over the same food. So one afternoon, I bumped into him in the gents. He was coming out of a cubicle blowing his nose. I said Malachy, you've got a constant cold, what's wrong with you? He sighed wearily.

Love.

He started washing his hands. Didn't use the dispenser. Ignored the hand-dryer.

Tells me six months ago he met a woman. Darina. They were instantly attracted to each other. This was head-over-heels variety. Not only was the sex great, eight times in one night, he claimed, and that was even before they got to bed, but they also had similar interests, a passion for the outdoors, browsing in bookshops and a quirky obsession with boogie-woogie piano players of the 1940s. He was never happier in his whole life. She even moved into his place after one week. This wasn't whirlwind, this was vortex!

A fortnight later however, he spotted a change. She became less responsive. Ardour cooled. Near arctic levels. She gave him queer and funny looks. This puzzled him. Then he noticed something. Her sinuses had cleared. When they first met she'd had a head cold. This got him thinking. Was there some connection? He sought advice.

'Pheromones.'

Malachy's friend and confidante, polymath and cheat at pub quizzes, Turlough Dexter knew a lot about things.

'They are what attract people to each other. The smell we emit attracts a mate. It's primal. It's nature.'

Turlough's theory was simple.

'It is quite obvious that when Darina met you she had an acute viral rhinopharyngitis, head cold to average Joe's like yourself. Her olfactory sensibility was all askew, she becomes inexplicably attracted to you, and from what I've seen of her, you are totally out of her league. Totally. Now, that her rhinovirus is clearing up, her sense of smell is returning, as well as her general common sense, and she realizes she is no longer attracted to your pheromones, in fact she is probably secretly repulsed by them.'

So Malachy needed to think fast. The love of his life was about to walk out his door. Change to a stronger cologne? Turlough said it wouldn't work. Shower four times a day? No effect on the pheromones.

'Pheromones are like scents of the sub-conscious and once the pheromonian equilibrium has been upset, it is only a matter of time before the relationship ends and heartache begins.'

This guy Turlough sounded like a bit of a jerk. Would be no friend of mine. As Malachy continued his story he started to scratch at his head until a small flour dust cloud of dandruff gently landed in the silver chrome washing basin below.

Basically, he realized his choices were limited. For their romance to survive and thrive Darina would have to come down with a common cold each week for however long they were together. And since Darina was the love of his life and he never ever wanted to let her go, this meant the rest of their God-given days. However, he was not deterred by this possibly decades long undertaking. He even coined his own term for it – The Malachy Mission.

Seeing himself as an inveterate man of action and problem-solver, he saw no obstacle in this illness-inducing, snot-centric enterprise and adopted all kinds of strategies as the months went by. A small incision in her shoes so the wet from the ground seeped in and she unknowingly walked around the streets in damp socks. Ingenious on his part, but she just got better and went out and bought a new pair of shoes.

Winter arrived. The season was Malachy's natural ally. He suggested they take public transport as much as possible, given their love of nature and grave concern about the future of the planet. Even if it meant, at peak times, people sitting opposite them and coughing in their faces. Darina agreed. This led to her being struck down for most of December with a particularly heavy strain of the coxsackievirus she picked up from a pair of wheezing identical twins in matching khaki anoraks.

Other ploys? Telling fibs about the immersion having been on. End result? She had tepid showers leading to another bout of the sniffles. Or leaving windows open. Another successful outcome, somewhat negated by that unfortunate burglary and theft of, amongst other items, their prized Meade Lux Lewis box-set. Begs the question. What 21st century burglar would steal a Meade Lux Lewis box-set?

Malachy's most devious and monstrous scheme was to remove her discarded mucous filled tissues from the bin and hide them under her pillowcase. Breathing in her own germs was a guaranteed way of prolonging her nasal turmoil indefinitely. I nearly got sick when he told me that one, I mean what else was in the bin? Did he do much rooting? I hope he wore latex gloves. On the disgusting human behaviour Richter scale? A definite nine.

No matter what he did, each time she eventually recuperated, which of course meant her sense of smell returned and she started to give him the queer and funny looks.

The pressure was becoming too much. The continuous maneuvering was taking its toll. He was going out of his mind. Also, *he* was constantly coming down with a head cold himself because of his proximity to her.

He looked at me.

'Being in love is a stuffed nose hell.'

As for the sex? Eight times a night had turned into no times a night. Nothing spelt disaster for an incipient orgasm like a violent sneeze.

Malachy shook his head and sighed. He had no idea what he was going to do. He was meeting Turlough Dexter later. I wished him well as he exited.

I didn't see Malachy around for a while. Then two months later I bumped into him in the elevator. He was looking very healthy.

'Malachy, how are things with Darina?'

'We got married. And look. No head cold.'

'How come?'

'It had nothing to do with the pheromones. One night she sits me down and says stop being such a slob and we can stay together. She'd give me those queer and funny looks because of my intermittent disgusting human behaviour. I tell you, I'm a changed man.'

He smiled, stopped picking at his ear and flicked a tiny ball of earwax through the opening elevator doors.

HECKLER FOR HIRE
(featuring Quasimodo O'Shaughnessy)

In late 2004 I started using a small dictaphone to record my stand-up routine. To monitor where laughs were coming in my material.

Ok, not laughs. Strained muffled pitiful groans.

One evening, I performed a spot at The Comedy Hovel. Later when I got home, I did what I always did. Grabbed a beer from the fridge. Locked myself in the bathroom. Assumed a foetal position under the sink. Cried for ten minutes. Composed myself. Played back the tape.

The aural torture this particular night was more agonizing than usual. I heard coughing and sighing (me), polite slightly confused murmurings (them), persistent low hum (fridge behind the bar), intermittent barking (guide dog of audience member) and finally, some snoring (them again or was it me)? Things had gotten so bad at this stage I couldn't honestly remember.

However this gig was also interspersed with comments from somebody sitting next to the dictaphone.

That somebody was Jason Best.

Hotshot young comedian Best, booked to close the evening, hadn't noticed the dictaphone placed side-stage earlier and had begun whispering comments about my routine.

A litany of stinging negative criticisms climaxed finally with a solemn declaration – 'Frankly, I don't think I've ever seen a worse comedian in the whole of my professional existence.'

The whole of his professional existence? Jason Best was nineteen-years-old!

And in my view, he represented all that was going wrong with stand-up comedy in the early years of the twenty-first century. Jogging on stage in a t-shirt, torn jeans and trainers with his boy band front man smile. How could anyone who was nineteen do a comedy routine? How could anyone that good-looking do a comedy routine? I'd always thought comedy was about being an ugly outsider.

Like me.

Quasimodo O'Shaughnessy.

(I was signing on the dole when starting off in comedy, so I had to come up with a stage name. This name just came to me in a dream. A very *strange* dream.).

I cursed Jason Best and swore I'd get my revenge.

The following week I was at a gig outside of town. Circuit veteran Harvey Forde's act was being continuously interrupted by a loud heckler. Harvey hated hecklers and spent his non-gigging hours stalking and verbally abusing former hecklers at *their* places of work but was having enormous difficulties with this heckler. That's when I came up with an idea. How about hiring this heckler to go to Jason Best's hugely anticipated high profile gig the following week?

I tracked the heckler down after the gig. Harvey Forde had him in a chokehold in a side alley outside. I intervened.

'Harvey, leave it. Heckling's part of the game.'

Harvey muttered something under his breath and went back inside.

I looked at the heckler. Round guy. Goatee. Red face. His name was Baz.

'I caught your heckling in there. I liked what I heard.'

He was chuffed.

'Thanks dude. Which bit in particular?'

'Get off the stage, you unfunny cunt. I like the hard-core stuff. I'm a traditionalist.'

'I don't know. I felt that was a bit predictable. I like to vary it. Try to be original. Sometimes I just go Warum?'

'What's that?'

'It's German for why. I call them my Zen heckles. It confuses the fuck out of some comedians. And there are so many crap ones.'

I nodded. Baz sighed and looked up at the sky.

'Imagine a world with no blow jobs.'

Puzzled, I looked at him. He went on.

'80% of stand-up comedians would have nothing to talk about. It would *almost* be a price worth paying.'

'Good point.'

'Comedians. Nothing but amplified needy people thirsting for affirmation from pissed idiots – 'toenails, what's that all about?' – is that funny?'

Yikes. That was one of my observations. I had a four-minute routine on the redundant toenail. Baz must have caught my act at some stage. Thankfully, he hadn't placed me yet. Attempting to abort him mid-rant, I moved the conversation on.

'Would you like to make some money?'

'What do you mean?'

'I'll pay you some cash to go to Jason Best's gig next week at The Tee-Hee-Hee Club and heckle the bejaysus out of him.'

'How much?'

'One hundred euro.'

'Brill.'

Baz grinned.

'Maybe I should get cards made up. Heckler for Hire.'

It was two days before Best's gig. I thought things over. Maybe I had over-reacted. So what if the Best kid thought my act was rubbish. My act *was* rubbish.

I decided to ring Baz and cancel things.

'Listen, Baz, I've had a change of heart. No matter how much you despise him, it's kind of unethical to try and ruin a comedian's act. And illegal. Pre-meditated heckles are considered sedition, I read somewhere. Sorry for wasting your time.'

Baz cleared his throat.

'I wasn't going to heckle him anyway. He offered me one hundred and twenty euro not to heckle him but to heckle you instead, next time you perform. I thought you looked sort of familiar.'

There was a pause.

'Was it you who did that piece of unfunny shit about toenails? '

'Uhm...'

I became flummoxed and enraged. Temporary legal rational forgiving me was history.

'Baz, you know what, heckling is too good for Jason Best. I want you to maim him. That cheesy-grin Timberlake face of his needs disfiguring. Immediately. Have you any friends... in that area... Baz?'

Baz wheezed.

'Maybe one or two. Oh, one more thing. He says, frankly, he doesn't think he's ever seen a worse comedian than you in the whole of his professional existence.'

Enter illegal *completely* irrational unforgiving me.

'You know what Baz. If you are going to go to the trouble of maiming him you might as well kill him. Eight hundred euro, Baz?'

'A grand.'

'Ok.'

After buying some new batteries for the dictaphone, checking my bank balance and contemplating how completely unsuited I would be to a modern day real-life recreation of *The Shawshank Redemption*, I called Baz again.

'Baz, that murder thing, forget it, I'll top his one

hundred and twenty, I'll make it one hundred and fifty euro just to heckle him. Are we clear on this, Baz? No homicide. Just heckle.'

'Whatever.'

The night of the gig, I paid Baz fifty euro up front so he could have a few beers and get in the mood. I only had one instruction.

'No 'warum'. Stick to the classics.'

But when Jason walked on and began his act, something came over Baz. He was silent. Almost child-like. Think 1858. Lourdes. Apparition time all over again. But no heavenly music in the background. Just monster laughs. Baz was simply in awe of the 'precocious, awesome, fierce comedic brilliance' – *The Irish Times* – and became convulsed with helpless laughter. He laughed so much he forgot he had to heckle. I reproached him.

'Baz, some heckling please!'

'Sorry, dude.'

Post-paroxysm Baz failed to stop his sides splitting. He was literally in pain. But happy pain.

I persisted with my request.

'Baz, some 'fuck off you unfunny cunts' please. I'm paying you for some 'fuck off you unfunny cunts'!'

'I'm sorry dude, this guy is, forgive the cliché, a comic genius!'

The crowd erupted at another one-liner. Baz looked at me.

'My brain is incapable of constructing a heckle in the presence of Jason Best. I just can't stop guffawing violently!'

Baz guffawed violently. On-stage Jason wiped some sweat from his brow. And went on with the show. In fact, he stayed on for *three* extra hours.

How much laughter can humanity take?

At the end of the night Baz approached me.

'Jeez, I'm exhausted.'

He shook his head in wonder.

'Frankly, I don't think I've ever seen a better comedian in the whole of *your* professional existence.'

Later that year Jason Best became a huge star. As for me, I dropped off the dictaphone at my local charity shop and myself and Baz came up with an offbeat business idea – the world's very first workshop for hecklers.

FATE WEARS A BLINDFOLD

My name is Clive. I'm six foot five. I have a glass eye. I look like a brother of the actor Steve Buscemi. Only much taller. By day I write film screenplays. By night I collect money for the mob. I am Manbag Bagman.

And right now I'm going to be killed.

All because of a dame.

Marja.

Polish for Maria. I call her Mire. As in quagmire. As in the Battle of the Somme. I wish she'd *been* a no-man's land.

I first met her a week ago. My boss, Ivor the Terrible sends me to Mountville Crescent, over on the Westside, to pick up a debt from Smalltime Limey. Smalltime Limey is a smalltime limey. Nicknames ain't what they used to be. There's so much idiocy in the world nowadays. Brainlessness Central. A planet of cretins.

When I get there, there's no sign of Smalltime. However she's there. A goddess behind a plume of smoke. Well, not that much smoke. Those e-cigarettes don't cut it as far as I'm concerned. She tells me Smalltime has taken a powder. Blown town. But somehow it doesn't ring true. Like Smalltime's hairpiece sticking out from that half-closed wardrobe door.

'I don't care what's going on sister, Smalltime owes

Terrible. Now hand over the dough.'

Suddenly she lunges forward. E-cigarettes on human flesh? Child's play. I push her back but with her left hand she's already navigating towards my genital quarter. Major Tom is aroused. Before I know it we're lost in a tsunami of animal passion. I hoist her on my cement bag thighs, up against that half-closed wardrobe door. I thrust. She shrieks. Major Tom to Ground Control. Commencing countdown engines on.

I withdraw after climax. She offers me an e-cigarette and Smalltime's hairpiece falls on my still erect member.

I start thinking. A man could do a lot with that dough. Like give him the time and space to develop as an artist. Finish a few of those screenplay ideas and start hitting the big time.

We divvy up the 20 G and go on the run.

An hour later, we stop off just outside Tyndale. We find a small place where we hole up for a day or two. This is what happiness is. I'm writing. She's smoking. And there is non-stop commencement of countdown engines.

One night in bed she thinks she hears something.

'Clive?'

'Yeh.'

'Is that like, your real name?'

'Yeh.'

'Maybe we should get out of here.'

'No need.'

'But what about Ivor the Terrible? Surely his men

will be after us.'

'No they won't. He's called Ivor the Terrible, because he is a terrible crime boss. He can't organize anything. He probably doesn't even know the money's gone. You let me do all the worrying, baby.'

I'm in love. And love does strange things to guys. Sometimes it hits you like a tornado. Other times it sneaks up on you like a tarantula. Marja is like a cross between a tornado and a tarantula. She is a force of nature with a rather small chest size.

She looks over at me one evening.

'What are you writing?'

'A screenplay.'

'What's it called?'

'*Fate Wears a Blindfold*.'

'Oh. Let me guess. About some guy's inability to control his destiny. That whole determinism versus free will stuff. Like some film noir. Sounds like old hat to me.'

This doll surprises me. A philosopher, huh? And she knows about film noir. Not many people do anymore. A guy I know once told me his favourite film noir was *Shaft*. There is so much idiocy in the world, nowadays. Brainlessness Central. A planet of cretins.

'So what's the film about?' she wonders.

I don't answer. I suddenly feel inferior in her company. I don't want her to think I lack depth as a writer. The screenplay is actually about a young girl called Fate who works in a circus and wears a blindfold during the knife-throwing act of her legendary father. The Great Daggero! Gee, maybe I'm wasting my time with this writing lark.

I re-examine my approach to my work. Maybe I should take something from my real life. Write what you know they say. Maybe about looking like Steve Buscemi's taller brother. With a glass eye.

Next morning I'm on a roll. In my cocoon of creativity. That happens when you write. Don't notice anything going on around you. Like when someone has a Mauser 7.65 in your face. I look up. It's Ivor the Terrible.

'Your vaping vamp was in touch. She got bored with you. Did a runner. Took the dough with her. We're going to have to kill you.'

I look over at Ivor's brother. Terry. The Terrible.

'Wait a minute!' I say.

But it's too late. A shot rings out.

I still think of Marja. She's the reason I quit writing. Dumped my manbag the day after I left hospital. Ivor didn't really shoot me in the face. More like the corner of the ear. Like I said, terrible at everything. I lead a normal life now. Well, sort of normal. I'm working for some lookalike agency.

Why would anybody be interested in hiring a nobody who looks like a tall Steve Buscemi with a glass eye?

Planet of cretins.

A PINT WITH OLD FRIEND ALAN

'Karl, do you think there's a warranty on last rites?'

'A warranty?'

'Yeh like, or a best-before-date.'

'I never thought about that.'

'I'm just asking because about four years ago Dad was unwell, very unwell, looked extremely poorly and pasty, breathing like a fog-horn, this looks like it we all thought, this has to be it, so we contact Fr Fogarty to come to the house.'

'Yeh?'

"'He's looking poorly' Fr Fogarty says, 'A very pasty pallor.' 'Time for the last rites?' I ask. 'Most definitely,' he replies. 'Normal unction? Run-of-the-mill unction or extreme unction?' I inquire. I was always well up on unctions. Fr Fogarty looks at me and says 'Not just extreme unction. I think your father needs some hardcore unction.' I didn't know they did one called hardcore unction. Anyway, we all look at each other standing around Dad's bed. We're all very worried. Fr Fogarty says 'I've got some communion wafers on me, always have a special supply just in case.' Fr Fogarty takes out what looks like a little golden snuffbox from his inside pocket and removes a pristine host. He starts speaking lowly in Latin, a singsong cadence and tries feeding the small circular wafer to Dad. Dad's mouth remains firmly closed. Trouble eating solids. Jessa Mae our Filipino care-worker has an idea. She whispers to me and asks me to run it by Fr Fogarty. 'I don't know if this would be ok, but we have garlic crusher, downstairs, would it be acceptable uhm... liturgically speaking to run the host through the garlic crusher?' Fr Fogarty ponders the matter. Dad wheezes ominously. 'Sure we'll give it a go. Time is of the essence,' he says. Jessa Mae runs down to the kitchen and quickly returns with the garlic crusher and a spoon. Fr Fogarty places the communion wafer in the small crushing area of the utensil and Jessa Mae turns it furiously. Squashed remnant of communion wafer is collected on the spoon. Fr Fogarty resumes his Latin and as Jessa Mae gently tries loosening Dad's firmly locked jaws, Fr Fogarty seizing on a brief opening gently slides the spoonful of Blessedness into Dad's mouth. Miraculously Dad recovered.'

'Alan, what a story. I loved the bit with the garlic crusher.'

'Dad went back to his life of snoozing while reading the newspaper, mowing the lawn and driving ungrateful family members to the airport. Until last week that is. When he came down with a dreadful bout of pneumonia. And that got me thinking. Do I contact Fr Fogarty once more and do we have to go through the same rigmarole again, without Jessa Mae obviously who went back to Manila six months ago, but I think that garlic crusher is still next to the rolling pin and the egg whisker in the bottom shelf of the left-hand drawer, or are we still covered by the previous last rites?'

'I have no idea.'

'Elderly parents are a nightmare.'

'Yeh.'

'Hmm.'

'So eh, I guess you didn't get round to reading those stories, huh.'

'Oh fuck. Sorry. What can I say? Dad got pneumonia.'

'Fortuitous timing.'

'What's that meant to mean?'

'Nothing. I just feel no one will ever read any of these fuckin' stories. Sorry about your Dad. I didn't mean what I just said.'

'It's ok. Look I promise I'll read them next week. Ok? Want another pint?'

'Guess so.'

'By the way. Did you ever think of crowdfunding?'

'What?'

'In case you don't get a publisher. It's all the rage now, Karl, for people in the Arts. To get things off the ground.'

'Nah. It's not my thing. You need to be young. By the time you get to a certain age in the creative world you've pretty much used up all the financial goodwill from your friends.'

'Just an idea.'

'Anyway, Bosco Reddin tried crowdfunding on FundMyBook for his book of poems. Ended up with minus seventeen pledges.'

SOME EXTRA STORIES KARL DIDN'T BOTHER GIVING ALAN SINCE HE HADN'T READ THE FIRST THREE

THE CARPENTER AND THE SNITCH
Joseph's Christmas Diary

(In the archaeological discovery of the year, Joseph the Carpenter's diaries have recently been unearthed. Here we examine his account of that very first Christmas and find a written testimony that at times gives us a surprising insight into this neglected biblical figure.)

DECEMBER 23rd — 9:43 p.m.

Things are quite tense with M. at the moment. We got into a blazing row after our pre-natal class. She asked me had I booked the accommodation for Bethlehem. I said yes. This was a lie. I was meant to tell the shepherd Shobal, the son of Ezer, who recently begat Azariah, to tell his brother Pharaz who runs The Room At The Inn Quality Budget Lodgings in Bethlehem to set something aside for us. But I forgot. There shouldn't be any problem though. I mean, it is a one-horse town in the back of beyond. It's just that I'd hate for M. to end up in the middle of nowhere having to give birth in some stable or something, but that's just my worried mind working overtime again. We'll be fine. Fingers crossed.

DECEMBER 24th — 7:56 p.m.

Arrived in Bethlehem. Finally. The roads were crazy the last hour, a donkey tailback all the way from Anathoth. To my eternal relief, there was one unoccupied room at The Room At The Inn. But M. wanted to look at it first. She wasn't impressed with it at all. Okay, there was that stale smell, and the mattress had seen better days and the towels weren't that fresh, but it didn't bother me that much. I guess because I'm a man and men don't notice these things. Well, that's what M. always claims, anyway. 'Let's take it!' I said, but M. disagreed. 'No, we'll get something better somewhere else.' That was three hours ago.

DECEMBER 24th — 9:52 p.m.

Have finally found the 'something better somewhere else.' To be honest, it's not perfect. In fact, my worst nightmare has come true: we *have* ended up in the middle of nowhere in some stable. I was going to launch into a long tirade about M. never taking my advice and that we should have stayed in The Room At The Inn but I felt it wasn't the right moment, with her waters having just broken. What do I do now?

DECEMBER 25th — 1:06 p.m.

I am a father. I can't remember much about the birth because I passed out during M.'s prolonged contractions. I'm gobsmacked that little old me, Joseph the Carpenter, is responsible for bringing this tiny creature into this world. Well, sort of responsible. I'm still not completely clear in my mind about the exact sequence of events all those months ago, and who exactly did what with my wife — and how — but I'm prepared to put all that to one side because this is a momentous day.

DECEMBER 28th — 9:18 p.m.

Felt a bit cooped up in the stable, so I went for a walk around Bethlehem. When I returned home, I noticed some loaves and fishes in the corner. I asked M. where she got them and she swore she didn't know. She told me she dropped off to sleep for a few minutes and when she awoke there they were. Later had a most satisfying meal. Must be something in the water 'round these parts, for it tasted just like wine.

DECEMBER 31st — 10:46 p.m.

New Year's Eve. Can't get to sleep with all the parties and revellers. It's louder than feeding time on Noah's Ark. We decide to have a quiet night in this year, having difficulty organizing a babysitter at such short notice. Anyway, M. said she didn't have anything nice to wear. Last year she spent hours getting ready. And then on her way out she turned to me and said, 'I hate myself in this crimson tunic. I look so fat!' Later we spent a rather strained evening with our friends Joachim and Jezabethum. Joachim is in the recycling business. He tells me recycled crucifixes are the future.

JANUARY 6th — 9:35 p.m.

I was in the middle of changing my first nappy this afternoon, when a voice said 'Hello.' I turned around and saw these three old guys just standing there with bags of stuff. From the word go, I didn't trust them. In life you always have to go with your initial instincts.

'Whatever you're selling, I'm not interested,' I said.

'No, you've got it all wrong.'

They then told me they were the Three Wise Men.

I called out to M. in a slightly sarcastic manner:

'Come here! I want you to meet the Three Wise Men. Not just ordinary men, mind you, but wise men.'

Then I really began to have fun with them.

'Well, we're the Two Tired Parents! What do you want?'

Then they started going on about the baby as they removed the stuff from the bags.

'We want to give you this.'

They showed me some gold, frankincense and myrrh.

'What's the catch?'

'No catch.'

Then they just turned around and left.

M. and myself looked at each other.

Something definitely not kosher about all this. Three old guys turn up out of the blue, and they want to give us stuff? M., being more naturally suspicious and paranoid in nature than me, came up with an angle.

'Maybe they are highway robbers,' she said. 'I mean those beards look like a joke, for starters. Maybe the authorities are after them and they're trying to dump the stuff somewhere, and later on they'll want to come back and cut our throats and retrieve it.'

She could be onto something. Then M. wondered, what happens in the meantime if we're found with the stuff? We'd be flogged, stoned, put away for years, and the kid would have to be taken in by social services. Where would that leave us all? And the future of Christianity? Without further discussion, we immediately disposed of the boodle in a well down the road. I'd never seen such fake looking merchandise anyway!

The Judas Journal

(Approximate translation of extract from Judas Iscariot's recently unearthed journal)

Am approached by a Roman centurion in a crowded bazaar. He asks me would I be willing to betray Jesus. It would be worth my while. He winks. I make an instant calculation. Eternal damnation or never having to hear another parable about sheep again. I decide to pursue the matter.

'How much you offering?'

'Thirty pieces of silver.'

Not bad. And anyway Rispah has been nagging me for weeks to buy her that new kethoteth. I look at the centurion.

'That sounds like a very interesting proposition.'

He wonders when I can do it. I tell him Thursday night. Jesus has organised this big get-together. Some supper thing. A thought crosses my mind.

'By the way, why do you need me in the first place? Why don't you just apprehend him yourselves?'

He sighs and shakes his head. Almost embarrassed. He states that although they have had Jesus under surveillance for the last number of years they have absolutely no idea what he looks like. He admits they fall down somewhat in that whole monitoring an individual and facial recognition area and it is something they definitely need to improve on in the future.

He suggests a plan. After our meal on Thursday night, he and a few of his soldiers will be waiting outside and he proposes that I should kiss Jesus for identification purposes.

Hold it right there, buddy.

'Did you say I have to kiss him?'

'Yeh. Those are the orders.'

'Can I not just point him out?'

'No,' he persists, 'You have to kiss him. Orders are orders. They come from above.'

He points to the sky. I'm confused.

'God?'

'No. Pontius Pilate, you idiot!'

I start to mumble.

'I feel uneasy kissing a man in public. Or in private for that matter. It's just something I wouldn't normally do.'

He grins.

'Come off it. Look what the Greeks got up to! Were you never in a Roman bath? Loosen up. Just one little peck.'

I bring up my parents.

'I'm sorry. I was brought up in quite a traditional household. That's all.'

He glares at me.

'Look Judas, there are guys out there who'd imbibeth his loins for thirty pieces of silver – all we're asking you to do is kiss him.'

I think about what he has said for a moment and realize he has put things in perspective. I agree to kiss Jesus.

Suddenly, it's Thursday night. We all turn up at the place. Newly opened. Gethsemane Nosh. Quite swanky and very busy. Jesus goes up to the maître d'.

'Good evening. A party of thirteen. Booked in the name of Christ.'

The maître d' consults his bookings scroll and sighs.

'Christ, is it? Let me see. No. I don't have the name here.'

Jesus looks at Peter. 'Did you book?'

No response. Jesus erupts.

'I can't believe this! Peter, how many times over the last week did I tell you to book! It's the Last Supper! It's so important that we have this meal!'

There is an awkward silence. The maître d' looks at us.

'I'll see what I can do.' He leaves.

'We can go somewhere else, Lord,' Bartholomew suggests.

Jesus shakes his head. He is getting agitated. Really starting to lose it.

'This time on a Thursday night? It is hopeless, Bartholomew! Most places will be all booked up.'

I'm secretly relieved. I have sixteen sweaty men in leather skirts hiding outside in a bush. I don't want us going anywhere.

The maître d' returns.

'I can fit you in, but I'll have to break you up into two tables of four and a table of five, is that all right?'

Jesus sighs. 'Well, I was hoping for a group table because I have some extremely important things to say that sort of determine the future of Christianity... but if it's the best you can do.'

We get three different tables in three different corners of the restaurant. I sit with Jesus, Peter, Andrew and Doubting Thomas in a poky little alcove next to the kitchen. Jesus is still shaking his head and muttering at Peter, who just stares straight ahead. Finally, Jesus calms down a little and asks for some bread and wine. Great! I could do with a glass. Ease this tension.

The bread and wine arrive.

'I think it's corked.'

It happens every time. When we go anywhere with that Doubting Thomas it's always the same story. There's always something. Andrew, the self-confessed sommelier of our group, sniffs at the wine.

'It's not corked. There's a hint of cinnamon, that's all. But it's a perfectly quaffable above average *vin de table*.'

Jesus picks up a piece of the bread. He taps at the side of his goblet as if about to make a speech. He clears his throat.

'Take this all of you, well, just the four of you'– he signals weakly at us – 'and eat it. For this is my body!' We look puzzled. Suddenly a bell rings loudly. Pandemonium. A fire has broken out in the kitchen. We are told to evacuate the premises. The emergency exit. Go out the back way. The back way! The perspiring pedites are still out front! What do I do? Do I kiss Jesus? Do I wait?

Five minutes later. We're outside. No sign of the leggy legionaries. Jesus addresses us.

'Look, let's just write off this evening. It hasn't worked out. The mix-up with the booking. The seating arrangements. The unfortunate blaze.'

He pauses.

'Can we re-schedule for next Thursday?'

THE SOMETHING OF SOMETHING

This is a story about a guy Giles, who knew a girl Janet, a long time ago. She had a boyfriend Fergus, but the guy and the girl would spend time together. He'd make her laugh. She particularly loved his Morrissey impersonation. One evening she gave him a lift home. When they arrived outside his flat, they sat silently in the front of her car. Was she waiting for him to kiss her? He didn't know. He never knew. Too scared to seize the day, to carpe the diem, he just said goodnight weakly as he fiddled with the car door handle and scurried out.

The years went by. She went to London to work in publishing. He did something vague in horticulture. They lost touch. Sometimes he'd think back on that moment when he didn't kiss her. Then one night, sitting in front of his computer, infused with red wine and middle-age ennui he Googled her name, and realized she'd moved back to Dublin. And lived close by. According to her website she operated her own proof-reading and editing services from home. Scrutinizing her photo, he noticed she had changed – then again he had changed, horticulture does that to you – but he still felt an attraction towards her. And she still had the same surname. Maybe she was single. Like he was. After a few long-term car crashes.

He devised a strategy. He would contact her under the guise of seeking professional expertise. To do some editing for him. Which meant he had to write a book. A book that needed to be edited – which meant an extra-long book. What could he write an extra-long book about?

Meeting someone was so complicated.

Apart from aspects of horticultural science and the core economic fundamentals of the agribusiness sector, his one area of expertise was Irritable Bowel Syndrome. He knew all about Irritable Bowel Syndrome. Personal reasons. But could he write a book about it? Of course not. He was no writer. Composing Christmas cards were a chore. There was no way he could create a mass of words, one after the other, in the right order that made some sense and kept a reader engaged. His world would always be a world of plant cultivation.

Then he remembered his old friend from college. Frank.

Frank spewed out trilogies. Sci-fi noir. Frank's very own genre. They were hugely successful online. About a space travelling private investigator Kevin Cosmos. 'Private eye of the stars – the ones in the sky, not Hollywood, dummy!' Frank's most recent book *Death Comes To Cosmos* had been picked up by some big name publisher.

The situation was explained over a smoothie. Frank was on his bi-annual detox.

'The longer the better, Frank. The more work she

has to do, the more consultations we'll have. This means more time to communicate with each other. Who knows where it will lead.'

'Giles, I think I have just the thing for this lady. Ever hear of Thomas Pynchon?'

'No.'

'He writes dense, complex novels. I went through my Pynchon phase when I was twenty-two. Wrote a 900 page novel called *The Something of Something*.'

'*The Something of Something*?'

'Yeh. She'll have her work cut out with that one.'

'Thanks buddy. Oh by the way, there's no porn or erotica in it, is there?'

'Of course there's porn and erotica in it. I was twenty-two.'

'Oh.'

'Hey, means to an end.'

Giles picked up the manuscript the following day. He'd unpacked fertilizer bags that were lighter. He hadn't planned to peruse *The Something of Something,* but when he did so became slightly worried about the porn and erotica content. After twenty impenetrable indecipherable indecent pages, he realized that if ever a book would ring the death knell to a prospective relationship *The Something of Something* would be that book. He could not give this book to Janet. More importantly he could not have the kind of girlfriend that got away thinking he wrote such sophomoric salacious drivel.

Why the book subterfuge in the first place, he thought in a moment of clarity while emitting loudly some not trapped, but incarcerated wind. Why not just email her? Or ring her? All her details were on her website. Better still, go to her local coffee shop and 'accidentally' bump into her?

It was a week later. He was sitting opposite Janet in Yet Another Coffee Shop, a newly opened place in town that advertised its very own blend of koala bear caressed Ethiopian beans. Or something like that. He had emailed her after all. But since he had decided to email her, he felt he really did need to give the proposed meeting a business pre-text. Hence, the bag of fertilizer sized package on the coffee table.

Who cares what she thought of the book. So what, about the porn and erotica. She worked in publishing. Must have come across all sorts of material. Anyway, Frank was right. Means to an end.

'I'm really impressed, Giles. I always knew you were artistic. '

'Thanks, Janet, for your support and kind words. Now remember, I did write it years ago. It's puerile, maybe a bit obscene in places and much too long. That is why I need your help.'

'Don't be over critical of your book. It's some achievement writing 900 pages.'

She looked at the cover page.

'Frank M. McFadden. Good pen-name.'

Giles had left Frank's name on the manuscript. Outwardly he remained calm.

Inwardly, he performed self-recrimination hari-kari.

They talked for some time. She told him she'd been married and divorced, had a son away in college in Sunderland and was enjoying life back in Dublin. He talked at length about arboculture, fogponics and mechanical weed control.

Coffee over, (the koala bear caresses had really made a difference) he offered to carry the manuscript to her car.

'Thanks, listen Giles, I'm going your way, have to pick up a few things. Can I drop you home?'

'Ok.'

Soon they were outside his small red mid-terraced house. Sitting silently in the front of her car. There was a long pause. A certain tension. Was she waiting for him to kiss her? After twenty-five years would he finally seize the day? Carpe the diem? He looked at her. Was about to lean over when there was a long powerful explosive sound.

Not trapped but incarcerated wind.

SISTERS ARE DOING IT FOR THEMSELVES

Small shop. Small town. Big problem.

I've only entered the cramped store to buy a packet of pastilles. On a whim, and with the help of the-pointy-finger-in-jacket-pocket manoeuvre, I've decided to rob it.

Bad move.

The shopkeeper fiddles with the till.

'Only fifty euro in here.'

She stares at me. Unfazed.

'Would you like to make some real money?'

Seems like such a harmless woman.

'What do you mean, real money?'

'Five grand. If you bump somebody off.'

'Who?'

'My sister. We don't get on. And some family issues remain unresolved.'

Right. The mother's died. She's left both of them the house in the will. But only one of them cared for mammy all that time while the other was off in Australia having fun. And the one that stayed at home isn't happy. Don't think I want to involve myself in this sibling intrigue.

'I think I'll just take the fifty euro. And hand over another packet of pastilles.'

'Sure, what sort of man are you at all, Colm Killeen? I knew your aunt's people. One of the Horgan family from outside Kilbeggan, wasn't she?'

I hate Ireland. You can never do anything, anywhere, without someone recognising you from seven parishes down the road. Ever wonder why there was never a great Irish road movie? Because the place is so fucking small. The protagonists would get to their final destination too soon. People would be leaving the cinema after forty minutes.

I try to reason.

'I'm crap at killing. When I was a kid, I had this pet hamster called Hasselhoff and it was sick and we couldn't afford to bring it to the vet and daddy said...'

'Arey, will you stop with your auld stories. The price of hitmen has gone through the roof. They're all in Dublin, that's where the demand is. Tell you what, I'll make it six grand to do her. I'm Maisie, by the way.'

Guess, you could say, I'm a passive man. Open to suggestion. And very low on cash. I need that dough.

It's a week later. I'm on a date with the sister. Tessie. Good looking. But she's had more facelifts than Mount Rushmore. We're at some secluded beauty spot near Kilnaboy. She's all lovey-dovey. Pawing me like an oversexed panther. Is that a gun in my pocket or am I glad to see her? It's a gun in my pocket.

For real this time.

Maisie has sourced it. From Gilhooly, the old IRA man.

Tessie licks my face and thinking about how I got into this mess I curse my love of pastilles.

She starts whispering in my ear.

'What do you think of Maisie?'

'She's ok.'

'I detest her.'

I turn to Tessie. I know what's coming. She's going to tell me she made some money while she was off in Australia having fun. And has put some away for a rainy day. A rainy day when a murder may be committed.

'She's an obstacle. She'll always be. And now that I've met you...'

She looks at me with big pleading eyes.

'I know, it's asking a lot, and we've only just met but would you kill her for me? There'd be a bit of money in it.'

I sigh.

'But, Tessie, I'm crap at killing. When I was a kid I had this pet hamster called Hasselhoff...'

Over the next few days, as I prevaricate with Hamlet-like aplomb, they both separately approach me with the same idea.

'If you don't want to do any bludgeoning, knifing or discharging of firearms, I completely understand. But listen, have you any knowledge of creating gas leaks? There's a gas heater in the living-room and my sister loves the auld telly late at night. I'm figuring if we could get that gas heater to leak, we could have the perfect untraceable homicide – slow death by carbon monoxide.'

These sisters are batty. I have to get away from them. No one needs money this badly. I lay low for a few days. Consider approaching my friends Pimple McNicol and Eejit Atkins and hearing what they think about my predicament. But then I remember what my mother once said to me – 'Never take advice from a fella named Eejit.'

Then, in a coffee shop in Kilmallock I hear a news report over the radio. The correspondent says the police aren't sure if the fire in the farmhouse, where the two female bodies were found was started deliberately. Or was just a tragic accident.

A deliberate tragic accident, perhaps.

I finish my coffee, promise myself never to commit robbery again and think, maybe it's about time I get myself another pet hamster.

THE KARL MACDERMOTT ARCHIVE PART THREE

TWENTY YEARS OF DIARY EXTRACTS FROM *MUSINGS FROM A RUT – THE KARL MACDERMOTT DIARIES*

Thursday April 15th, 1996

Saw Gloria Gaynor last night on the television. She'd packed on a few pounds. Maybe she should re-name herself Gloria Weight-Gaynor. She was singing 'I Will Survive'. I thought to myself, if she keeps putting on all that weight that's not necessarily going to be a given.

Tuesday June 24th, 1997

I was supposed to meet my friend Alan today for a drink. Except he didn't want to drink. He told me he'd drank too much last night. The same thing happened last week when I met another friend Marcus, we were meant to go for a few drinks but when he turned up he told me he'd only be drinking water because he'd drank too much the night before. Last month Rachel and I had Tadgh and Orla over for dinner. The bottle of red wine and the bottle of white wine were already opened. They declined to drink any alcohol, apologizing profusely and saying they'd been out drinking until the early hours of the morning. That got me thinking. I have to ask myself, why do most people need to drink the night before they've arranged to meet me? At least Oliver never lets me down. My favourite drinking companion. Or as he calls himself Oh! Liver. Meeting him on Friday.

Friday June 27th, 1997
Oliver has just rang. He's off the drink. Doctor's orders.

Sunday October 11th, 1998
In my house when I was growing up, being politically correct meant voting Fianna Fáil.

Wednesday August 8th, 2001
These are some of the questions that kept me awake last night. Do creases from pillow-cases cause wrinkles? Can a corner boy be anywhere or does he specifically need to be adjacent to a perpendicular structure? How come they never update the songs they play in ice-cream vans? When did they start calling industrial estates business parks? When was salad cream usurped by mayonnaise? When did tennis players stop drinking Robinson's Barley Water? Why is it that photos of politicians wearing sun-

glasses look as odd as photos of young children wearing sunglasses? A person's ear grows 2mm per decade after the age of thirty. If science is right and at some future date we all end up living to one-hundred and twenty, will we all start looking like Spock from *Star Trek*? If you're scared of dogs and you go blind can you get another animal to be your guide? Do sheep count humans when *they* try to get to sleep?

Friday June 7th, 2002

By nature I'm a cautious pessimist.

Saturday November 1st, 2003

How come it never rains on the night of Halloween? I mean what are the chances of every 31st of October being dry? But it never rains! Which means, firstly you have to hide under the kitchen table when the kids in their costumes ring your front door offering to trick and treat and then when that problem subsides you have to listen all night long to the fireworks!

Monday February 23rd, 2004

Sometimes I wish I owned a car. Especially when the time comes to dump bottles at the bottle bank. I have to walk clatter-clank-clatter-clank with a heavy bag, clatter-clank-clatter-clank down the street, clatter-clank-clatter-clank where I always bump into a neighbor, clatter-clank. Turning into Hiberno-Hugh Grant, I cough embarrassedly and mutter 'Actually, it's not as bad as it seems. There are numerous olive oil bottles in there. Myself and Rachel strictly adhere to a Mediterranean diet.'

Friday May 19th, 2006

Why is it that every time you go to the airport and you are stressed and you need to use the toilet, that is always the precise time the cleaning staff are in there.

Monday June 19th, 2006

Nervous breakdown? Not all it's cracked up to be.

Friday August 18th, 2006

This afternoon I saw an attractive woman pick up a second-hand edition of *Return of the Navajo Android* in the Oxfam shop on Parliament Street. I wrote *Return of the Navajo Android*, a 700 page dystopian eco-fable in 1998. It was well regarded in certain circles (select but odd circles, ok, crank geek circles) after novice publisher Unputdownable Books took a chance with it. (Their only book to date). The woman looked at it for a minute, read the flap jacket, saw my picture – God, I was so good looking back then, a blond, freckled Clooney in a polo-neck – but then she just put it away. I sighed. It's the problem living authors of extremely modest profile face every single day when their novel is picked up by a prospective buyer in a bookshop. The whole 'who-in-the-name-of-God-is-this-nobody-if-he-was-any-good-I'd-have-heard-of-him' problem. Now if the author is dead sixty years that changes things. It becomes a 'who-in-the-name-of-God-is-this-obscure-long-dead-nobody-could-be-an-interesting-discovery' scenario. In other words, obscurity + the present = penury. Obscurity + time = a possible sale.

Monday November 20th, 2006

Had a meeting with my agent Sisyphus O'Shea today. He says screenplays are where the money is. He's come up with a screenplay idea that he wants me to work on. It has a terrorism angle and is about a guy from the Middle East with profound identity issues. He already has the title. *Osama Sinatra*.

Wednesday April 11th, 2007

Can a bald man be true to his roots?

Saturday September 8th, 2007

While standing at the bar in Grogan's tonight waiting to

order a pint, the poet Bosco Reddin, sitting on a stool, turned to me and asked 'Is it better to be a has-been or a permanent never was?' He then tried to sell me his latest collection of poems *Hailstones in June*.

Friday April 25th, 2008

There's a beauty to life. There's a futility to life. Life is beauty-futility.

Sunday July 13th, 2008

Was talking to Alan today. He's quit his job as a music journalist for *Hot Press*. He told me he is getting too old. He feels, as he puts it, 'demographically exiled'. Not only is he unfamiliar with the young singers he is meant to interview, like Thrush Dweeb, Chantal Epoch, Rufus Toyboy or Tiny Tweezer, but he is also unfamiliar with the people they cite as influences. He told me that he wants to be a voice-over artiste. I wished him luck and told him that a voice-over artiste is merely an actor who doesn't suffer from Tourette syndrome or is in a coma.

Thursday February 12th, 2009

Charles Darwin was born two hundred years ago today. My position on Darwin is this. He made right monkeys of us.

Saturday October 17th, 2009

Went out with a group of friends for a meal last night. I ended up sitting at the end of the table, so anytime the waitress was topping up the wine glasses from yet another bottle of over-priced Chablis, the bottle had already emptied by the time she got to me. Life is all about where you are at a particular moment.

Wednesday February 10th, 2010

Neighbours and blood relatives are very similar. People you'll never really know that well, who you happen to be thrown together with, during your journey through life. I noticed my neighbour walking home ahead of me today. He is a very slow walker. But he is also a painfully reticent conversationalist. Even worse than me on the small talk scale. So to avoid trying to talk to him as I walk with him I had to lessen my walking pace and secretly follow him without overtaking him. Took me one-and-a-half hours to get home. Yesterday, I saw another neighbour. I went out of my way to say hello to her. She ignored me. But I think she accidentally ignored me. As opposed to intentionally ignoring me, which is what she would normally do. She wasn't expecting to see me on that street in that part of town, so she hadn't prepared herself for ignoring me. I usually try to ignore most people but with her, because she completely ignores me, I make a special effort to always greet her. Just to make her feel uncomfortable. But she usually ignores me.

Monday May 10th, 2010

Sometimes I feel my life is one long Laurel and Hardy movie where I'm both Laurel *and* Hardy.

Saturday August 28th, 2010

I heard someone talking about Viktor Frankl's *Man's Search for Meaning* on the radio last week so today I went into my local bookshop and uttered a sentence I was most proud of. 'Do you have Viktor Frankl's *Man's Search for Meaning* because I am a man and am in search for meaning.' The pony-tailed guy behind the counter, who looked like a failed roadie, consulted his computer, said 'sorry, my man,' and then, rather than suggesting he order the book for me, proposed I order it myself from Amazon. Bookshops are doomed. Later, I did some browsing. Giggled at the risible staff recommendations on the far shelf. I don't care if you found *On Chesil Beach* taut and judiciously executed, Tristan! Finally picked up a Tallulah Bankhead biography for two euro.

Thursday January 6th, 2011
I used to have nervous energy. Now, all I have is nervous lethargy.

Friday June 3rd, 2011
Alan has been pressuring us all week to catch his one-man show on the legendary American rock critic of the 1970s, Lester Bangs, at the Project Arts Centre. So, myself and Rachel went last night. We walked in and were pleasantly surprised by the large number of expectant audience members in the foyer. But when the show was announced we realized most people were there to see the other show that was on upstairs. We were the only two who ended up going to see *Unexpurgated Bangs*.

Wednesday October 19th, 2011
A vast majority of people in the Arts, leading the creative life, survive on tiny triumphs. An article here, a run in a play there, a commission here, some TV work there. Nothing but tiny triumphs. And one survives on those tiny triumphs. Not necessarily financially. But spiritually. They keep you going. But as you get older the gap between achieving one tiny triumph and another becomes larger. Whereas when you were thirty you may have had three tiny triumphs in one year, by the time you hit your late forties, the tiny triumph becomes like a bus

timetable after nine o'clock at night. This is the lot for nearly everyone working in the Arts. Of course there are the exceptions. People with actual careers. Meryl Streep. Martin Amis. Red Hurley. But for the rest of us – it's just a matter of clinging to those tiny triumphs.

Saturday March 10th, 2012

About six months ago we began to have a noise problem. Every night we heard something play the maracas in our cavity wall. Then move up to our attic and practice for the Olympic 100 metres until dawn. 'Maybe it's just a mouse,' Rachel said hopefully. 'Not with that noise,' I replied. 'A mouse I can live with,' she continued. 'A mouse is scary but kind of cuddly. A rat? Scary but kind of bubonic.' I sighed. 'Only one way to find out.' The next morning after extensive research online – 'mouse droppings look like poppy seed, rat droppings are MUCH LARGER' – I unfolded the underused attic stairs and made my way up. MUCH LARGER. We set a trap, put a piece of cheese on it and waited. Nothing happened. He didn't like the cheese. Thinking maybe he was a discerning foodie rat, we purchased more upmarket cheese, re-set the trap and waited. (Notice the way I just wrote the words 're-set the trap' as if it is the most run-of-the-mill and casual thing one could do – it's not. It is an extremely scary task where you suddenly become very attached to your (still) attached fingers as you warily release the trap while carefully placing a new piece of bait in position and yanking the trap back again hoping it won't snap.) The more upmarket cheese didn't work either. Ok, he doesn't like cheese. Maybe a bit of fat from some ham. We re-set the trap again (more potential loss of finger related torment) and waited. Nothing. Maybe this rat is on a diet. Or watching his cholesterol. We decide to fork out too much money for some professional who will put down some poison. He turns up in a van. 'Environmental Services' plastered on its side. At least he's discreet. Not like the one that turned up for a neighbour a few years back. 'Rodent Extermination Inc.' with a picture of an expired rat on its front bonnet. Rob, his name was Rob – apt with the prices he was charging – climbs up to the attic, puts some poison pellets in small plastic trays arranged where he thinks our unwanted guest gets in, charges us a hundred euro and says he'll be back in a few days. He claims the rat will eat some of the pellets, get dehydrated, leave the attic and go outside to seek water. Eventually he will die a lonely death somewhere. I have to be honest and say I do not feel the remotest sympathy about this eventuality. The few days go by. The nightly noise and mayhem continues, but when Rob returns, the poison pellets remain untouched. First time it's happened in twenty years Rob says. Give it another while. We give it another while. A month. Still nightly noise. Ring Rob. No answer. Ring Rob again. Leave message. Then another message. Then yet another message. Finally get to talk to Rob. Listen, I've done my part he says. I can't legislate for this rat. You said he won't touch cheese. Won't touch a bit of fat. Won't go near my pellets. The only other thing I can think of is one of those ultra-sound alarms. Two more weeks elapse. More maracas. More 100 metre sprints. More insomnia. We decide – ok, more financial outlay. For the ultra-sound alarm. And of course for the electrician to install it. His name was also Rob. Apt. Again. He explains while up in the attic installing the device that the ultra sound alarm emits a sound that only certain insects and mice and rodents can hear, and once they hear it, it drives them absolutely insane and they have to get away from the source of the sound as soon as possible. We simultaneously nod as we avert our eyes from his hairy builders crack. All that money he charges and he can't afford a proper belt, we think. Or braces – why doesn't he wear braces? – go for the retro-tradesman look. Why is it always obligatory to be exposed to the tops of their hirsute bottoms? That was two months ago. The ultra-sound alarm didn't work either. The rat must be old, Rachel thinks. He's a fussy eater, has acquired wisdom with age by not touching the pellets but is also hard of hearing. So we're stuck with this old guy. Set in his ways. The permanent rodent.

Friday June 8th, 2012

Many years ago my mother turned to me and said 'You haven't done a day's work in your life.' 'Au contraire,' I replied. 'September 10th, 1981.' September 10th, 1981 was my only ever day of gainful employment. In Dunnes Stores, Eyre Square, Galway. Packing tin cans on supermarket shelves. 'So this is what real people do, I thought. Sod it, who wants to be a real person.' I lasted until lunchtime. Didn't return after my break. The famous words of Dr Martin Luther King Jr. popped into my head as I ran down Williamsgate Street that afternoon. 'Free at last! Free at last! Thank God almighty, I'm free at last!' I was reminded of all this yesterday as I placed my shopping (including two tin cans) on the conveyor belt in the Dunnes Stores branch of the Stephen's Green Shopping Centre. A Spanish woman behind the check-out started scanning my items. When she was finished, she looked up and asked me in a strong Castilian accent 'Do you have Dunce card?'

Wednesday July 11th, 2012

Had another meeting with my agent Sisyphus today. He's got this idea that, once more, he wants me to work on. It's an idea for a TV series. He plans to try to sell the show to HBO or Showtime or one of those premium American cable networks and he says that if it works out I could be the 'showrunner'. I kept a straight face. The series is about a very stupid accidental serial killer who in each episode, through no fault of his own, ends up killing someone. As always, all Sisyphus has at the moment is the title of the show. *Blood is Thicker than Walter.*

Monday November 19th, 2012
I've spent my whole life pushing the *wrong* buttons!

Tuesday December 11th, 2012
The American writer and maestro of smug pomposity Gore Vidal once said 'Every time a friend succeeds I die a little.' I've seen so many friends succeed I must be decomposing within. It's official. I'm 61% dead. Let me see, there was Ronnie Wall, who became lead singer of The Sinister Mannequins, a top Goth act in the UK in the late 1980s. They had a huge hit in 1989 with the single 'She's a Tennis Star Groupie'. The only song in the history of pop to rhyme Gerulaitis with cystitis. Adrian Crosby got his break acting in that post 9/11 HBO drama, *Altitude.* Another mate Anthony Kirwan went to MIT in Boston and popped up three years ago with a best-selling self-help and how to make loads of money book, *Pole Vaulting in Flip-Flops – How to Overcome Obstacles, Locate Your Inner Awesomeness and Become a Key Influencer!* When it isn't my friends, it's the kids of my friends – that counts double Mr Vidal! – one of them, Dominic, became a start-up

sensation at some top conference in London by introducing an app called Skip App. If you are too mean to pay to dispose of your old chairs, 501's, David Lodge novels or Scritti Politti LP's, you can download Skip App and it will tell you where all the household skips in your surrounding area are located. Then in the darkest of night you can drive around the corner, open your car boot and offload your past. Such a great idea. What about domestic pets, Mr Vidal? That counts triple! My former next-door neighbour Rhonda's distinctly odd-looking poodle Rasputin, became the face of Poodle Power, an all-purpose eco-friendly detergent which has become the biggest selling cleaning agent in Germany over the last two years. This thing just keeps getting worse and worse. And now I've just read in the business section of *The Irish Times* that my old drunken friend, and now committed teetotaller Oliver has become a highly successful businessman tourist operator. He's come up with this idea that has taken off internationally – The Misanthrope's Tour Guide. It is geared towards the tourist who is looking for something different when he or she is going on a walking tour guide in a certain city. Negativity and cynicism about the place they are visiting as opposed to cringe-worthy smiles and endless positivity. Oliver has personally handpicked eight curmudgeons of either sex (equal opportunity misery – he did approach me last year to be one of the curmudgeons but I thought he was joking) to go around the tourist haunts of Dublin every day and basically slag the place off and insult the tourists and wonder why the hell did they waste their money and decide to visit such a dump. The feedback has been phenomenal! Social media is in overdrive. Other operators from different capital cities around the globe have been in touch with him. They want to replicate the idea worldwide under the brand name 'Misery Tours International'. He is tipped to become a billionaire by the New Year. Must re-calculate my figure, Mr Vidal. Yes. 73% dead at this stage. At least.

Thursday January 10th, 2013

Rachel recently commented about things being remarkably quiet in the house of late. I concurred. This morning we were greeted by a pungent smell emanating from behind the fireplace in the living-room. The permanent rodent is not so permanent now. Later, in our back garden, forced to have an unlikely al fresco meal in the severe chill of early January, Rachel turned to me and said 'I guess he just wanted to die at home.'

Monday February 18th, 2013

I went to the recently opened Titanic Museum in Belfast last week. Afterwards in the canteen, I was astounded to find that the only salad on offer was one containing Iceberg lettuce.

Friday April 5th, 2013

Walking down Quay Street in Galway this afternoon, I saw Carina Downing. Carina taught me a very important lesson about life many decades ago. I was a year ahead of my sister in our first National school. And when I was six years old and my sister was five, one day she got into a fight with one of her classmates. So the following day, at break-time, donning the mantle of a true big brother defender, I told my sister that I would settle matters with this girl. I asked my sister the name of the girl. She said, 'Carina Downing.' I said 'Where is she?' My sister pointed to a freckled piece of white string talking to a group of other girls in the school playground. So I approached the group of girls, and staring at Carina, I said, 'Carina, whatever problems you have with my sister, you can take up with me.' She said 'Ok.' And then suddenly with a peerless left hook that would have impressed Joe Frazier, she floored me. The lesson I learned about life that morning is never *ever* fight someone else's battles. You will end up with a nose bleed, a swollen ear, and a black eye for five days.

Wednesday June 3rd

I spend so much time loitering *without* intent.

Thursday July 11th, 2013

Bumped into the poet Bosco Reddin in the urinal of The Long Hall last evening. He turned to me and began, what is known in our world, as a Bosco rant. 'Bad stuff dates better than good stuff. Music. Movies. TV. Literature. Bad stuff just dates better. If something is considered mediocre or bad fifty years ago, chances are nowadays some critic, or people in general, will find it 'quaint' or 'kitsch' or 'so bad it is good', whereas if something was considered excellent fifty years ago people nowadays look at it and think 'this was considered great fifty years ago? It is terribly predictable and dated.' My point being, if you are in the creative world and you have your eye on posterity, produce mediocre to poor work!' He then sighed triumphantly. 'I know I do.' Then, with his left hand, he began shuffling in his corduroy jacket pocket and produced a small book with a pristine cover. 'That said, could I interest you in my new poetry collection *Popinjay's Lament*?'

Sunday August 25th, 2013

It's the height of the GAA season. I read something interesting about that recently. In early 1958, American comedian Jackie Mason, English comedian Ken Dodd and a ventriloquist's dummy from Clare engaged in a bizarre threesome. Nine months later, in an event that still confounds the world of science, Marty Morrissey was born.

Wednesday February 26th, 2014

Comedian Bill Hicks is dead twenty years today. Just another member of the dying young club. James Dean. Jim Morrison. Kurt Cobain. David Foster Wallace. People love people dying young. The cultural commentators. The media. Eventually, even the fans. However, the people doing the *actual* dying young probably don't like it as much.

Wednesday August 20th, 2014

When we visited the funeral home to make arrangements after my father died, the woman in the funeral home said, 'I recognized your dad. He was someone you'd see around the place.' Today I saw a poster for the late singer-songwriter Martin Fagan, announcing an up-and-coming tribute night for him. I didn't know him personally but he was 'someone I'd see around the place.' And that got me thinking that, at the end of the day, we are all just people who other people see around the place who end up being people who are no *longer* seen by other people around the place.

Tuesday April 12th, 2015

Because of my tight upper trapezius problems and ongoing issues with my sternocleidomastoid muscles, I was assigned via the public health system a physiotherapist in

St James Hospital. In popular culture one usually imagines a physiotherapist as a man or woman of boundless enthusiasm, vim and vigour. Not Colman. Just my luck, I get the one guy working in the whole physiotherapy industry who is decidedly low energy. Slightly bored. Listless. Possibly depressed. When he half-heartedly felt my occipital area ten minutes into our session, I swear I heard him wheeze.

Thursday October 8th, 2015

Monaghan poet Patrick Kavanagh once said, in the 1950s, that Dublin had a standing army of 10,000 poets. Nowadays that can be replaced with 1. Film-makers. 2. Stand-up comedians. 3. Bearded baristas. I have a meeting with Rufus Callagy, a young film-maker today. He wants to adapt one of my stories, *Colourful Horses,* and make it into a short film. The story is about a man who tries to find himself by buying a ticket for a carousel ride but he ends up just going round in circles. Rufus told me there could be some money in it for me if he gets the necessary funding from the Film Board. I agreed to meet Rufus but I insisted on meeting in the seated area of a Maxol service station off the N3 near Mulhuddart. Rufus wondered why I want to meet in such an unlikely place. I told him I live near-by. That is a lie. The real reason, and it is something I've learned from experience, is never ever have an appointment about a creative venture in a location which is on your route to or from town. Because when nothing comes of the appointment – sorry, Rufus, I don't hold out much hope for this one – every time you pass by that coffee shop or bar you will be reminded of another failed artistic endeavour. Whereas if you pick a place you will never return to like a Maxol service station near Mulhuddart, at least if things don't pan out you will not re-live your disappointment over and over again. People say I'm negative. I'm just a realist.

Tuesday May 3rd, 2016

I can't believe it is already early May. Nowadays, each year imitates life. Starts off slowly, builds momentum, moves faster and faster, and finally elapses. Or like the quickening momentum of holidays abroad. Despite my constant griping, I've always been obsessed with the passing of time. I have it on good authority – my mother – that my very first spoken sentence was 'Where does the time go?' I was Three-years-old. Time is like an espresso – it's here, it's gone. Where does the time go? Somewhere in the back of my head I keep thinking 1957 is twenty-five years ago. Where does the time go? So many of the poets, literary writers, philosophers, artists, over the centuries have asked that question, in all those works of art, without ever coming up with a satisfactory answer. Where does the time go? Fuck it, tempus fugit. Where does the time go? Isn't it time Boy George started calling himself something else? Where does the time go? Why is 'it's downhill from here' a negative expression? Shouldn't going downhill be a pleasant sensation? Where does the time go? When all is said and done, much was said, not much was done. Where does the time go? Most of the things I've known and loved and most of the people I've known and loved seem to be disappearing in a rear-view mirror. Where does the time go? Two nagging queries for the middle-aged man. Does my belly look big in this? Is this my penultimate passport? Where does the time go? Life is a beginning, a muddle and an end. Where does the time go? My grandmother is dead forty-four years. I remember the morning of her funeral. I was so thrilled. A day off school. But I do recall during the meal afterwards, looking around and noticing my parents and aunts and uncles seeming quite solemn. And I remember thinking to myself, 'This stuff doesn't really concern me. I'm only eight.' Then I poured myself another glass of Fanta. Where does the time go? When you can vividly remember something that happened forty-four years ago, you know the clock is not your friend. Where does the time go? Your fifties is the decade of the bendy country road. You never know what's 'round the corner. Where does the time go? When do you stop 'becoming' and just 'are'? Where does the time go? When does your destiny become an ex-thing? Where does the time go? The grave yawns. It's not going anywhere. From what age do you start asking that question, 'What song will I have played at my funeral?' Where does the time go? I started writing this diary entry nearly an hour ago. Where does the time go?

ONE FINAL MEETING WITH SISYPHUS

'Lovely to see you Karl. I have been pre-occupied the last few weeks, come in. Sit down. Sit down. Now Fidelma, like myself, hasn't got round to reading any of the stories yet, but hang on, hang on, none of that long face now, none of that long face, she's found out about a competition, closing date end of this month, first prize a thousand euro – The Lidl Short Story of The Year Award.'

'Lidl!'

'Stop it. Stop it. Be great coverage if you won it. She'll read the stories this weekend and decide if one is suitable for the competition. Now there is a small matter of an entry fee, eh fifty euro, that will need to be covered but sure we can discuss that again, closer to the date, once we have decided which story to enter.'

'What next? The Pound Shop Novel of The Year Award?'

'Look it, we're doing our best. What about a thank you Sisyphus for being in the loop? For having the auld lowdown. It is something to work towards, alright? Now I've a bit of other news as well. I know this fella Jens from Curious Lemon Productions, independent television producers, now they're working on a reality TV show. They filmed six weddings last year and they have followed six bridesmaids who caught the bouquet after the ceremony over the last while to see how they are getting on, romantically. They are calling the show *Bridesmaid Revisited* and RTE are just creaming themselves waiting to put it out. Nine-thirty Sunday nights. Advertising gold.'

'Waugh must be turning in his grave.'

'You know what they say – All's Fair in Love and Waugh.'

'Uh-huh.'

'You know, Karl, when you make a so-called witty aside you think it's fuckin' hilarious, but when I say something in that vein you never think it's funny.'

'Because it's not that funny.'

'Suit yourself. Now, they are looking for a writer.'

'What kind of writer?'

'Someone to write the links.'

'What do you mean?'

'You know, things like 'After meeting her mother over a coffee and brioche, Audrey goes and gets a pedicure in Ballsbridge before that big date with Clifford.''

'For fuck sake, Sisyphus.'

'This is money in the hand. Sure jays, even I could write it.'

'Well feel free, then. You write it.'

'I'll be honest Karl, I'm getting tired of this whole game. This whole SOS Management thing. I'm thinking of packing it in. Cassie Foy went with Lisa Richards. I've no clients left apart from yourself and you're a fierce difficult bollocks.'

'Excuse me?'

'I've been losing interest over the last few years. Heart isn't in it anymore. Sure look, I didn't even read those stories from *Snapshots of Incontinence.*'

'Inconsequence.'

'Exactly. And I'd have a better chance selling a penny-farthing at a motor show than a book of short stories in today's marketplace. You think auld Sisyphus O'Shea is just another cute hoor with his 1980s mullet and his big red Sligo face, but I'm just trying to survive like the next fella. And I'm sorry to say this business is dying.'

'What are you driving at?'

'Well every time I suggest something to you, you just turn your nose up at it.'

'No, I don't. Not all the time. '

'Well I'm tired of it. I don't have the energy anymore.'

'But what will *I* do?'

'Here's a suggestion. Stop fuckin' writing and get a real job.'

'But I can't stop writing. It's who I am. I've still so much left to say.'

'Arey, will you fuck off with bells on! You've got *nothing* to say. Or nothing *new* to say. And if you had something new to say, they wouldn't want it anyways.

All they want is something that reminds them of something else that has already been successful.'

'Where did all this come from? What's going on?'

'Arey it's not just you. On top of everything, the auld internet has changed people's habits. There are no readers anymore. Only scavengers. Content scavengers. People who spend their whole day in front of a computer skimming or scanning material. Then sharing the material or sneering at the material. The whole skimming, scanning, sharing and sneering generation. It's all over, Karl. The flag's been flying long enough. Time to take it down.'

'I can't believe this, Sisyphus. What's happening? This is like a bolt out of the blue.'

'Listen, I'm not packing it in as of this minute, we're still examining a few avenues with the various projects and ideas, but in the long term I think it's time you started thinking about finding new representation. Alright? Right, I'll see you Karl, I'll be seeing you. And look it, one final bit of advice. You never listen to auld Sisyphus, but will you ever change the flippin' title of that book you're working on, will ya? For Jesus sake! Come up with something that sticks out. Something like *Pilates With Penguins* or *Tapas With Llamas* or... something with turnips in the title. I've always found anything to do with turnips hilarious!'

THE LIDL SHORT STORY OF THE YEAR ENTRY

MEMOIRS OF AN UNLIKELY REBEL

Of all the obscure minor characters unearthed during the 1916 commemorations, none has a more interesting story than Old Ira Members. Old Ira Members was an old IRA member, the only orthodox Slovak Jew in the GPO in Easter 1916. I was fortunate enough to meet Old Ira once in Flatbush, New York in September 1993 while working on his proposed biography *Memoirs of an Unlikely Rebel*. Though nothing came of the biography, the transcript of my interview with him reveal a man, still lucid in old age who had some very interesting insights into the major and minor players of the 1916 Dublin Easter Rising. I started the interview by commenting on the fact that the previous week he'd had a high profile visitor from Belfast.

'Yes. Gerry Adams was here last week,' Old Ira announces as he gets out of his chair to greet me.

'I had one piece of advice for him. Never wear a yarmulke under a balaclava. Causes itchy scalp. He just looked at me blankly. Told me he'd never even been in the IRA. I didn't know what to say.'

Staying on the topic of the present day I wonder does Old Ira agree with the current Republican strategy of the armalite in one hand and the ballot box in the other.

'The what? Kosher marmite in one hand?'

'Armalite, honey. Armalite,' a voice pipes up from the kitchen.

Old Ira's wife, Nora, enters with a tray of tea.

'He loves kosher marmite. You can get anything in New York.'

The formidable Nora. Originally from Mayo, she has been involved in the cause on this side of the Atlantic for over fifty years.

'You could say I put the Nora in Noraid,' she jokes. 'Ira's hearing isn't the best any more. And sometimes he gets a little confused. Last week he started talking about a united Ireland and reuniting the thirty-eight counties, the thirty-two in the South and the six in the North and I said no Ira, no sweetheart, you got the number wrong but he's still my Ira and still as handsome as ever.'

I agree that he does look remarkable for his age. Old Ira beams.

'Ninety-seven in November, but everyone tells me I don't look a day over ninety.'

We settle down and I have a sip of my tea. I survey the living-room. A sacred heart of Jesus with a Jesus looking remarkably like Bobby Sands to a menorah in the colours of the Irish flag are just two of the items that grab my attention. I follow the sip with a gulp.

'Tell me about your early life, Ira?'

'I was born in part of the old Austro-Hungarian Empire, now part of Slovakia, in about 1895. A place called Pogromia. This place Pogromia was called that because all the people who had fled pogroms ended up there. My family were modest people. Humble people. Kept to ourselves. We led a frugal existence.'

'Times were tough?'

'Yes, and to overcome this we sold frugals. Poppa was always coming up with ideas. We went into the frugal business.'

'Frugals? What were frugals?'

'Fruit Bagels. Frugals! Get your frugals! Get your frugals! Every morning he'd be in the village square, unfortunately nobody wanted them. I still have Poppa's old recipe. Nora makes them somctimes.'

I look at Nora. She smiles.

'I made some this morning. Would you like to try a frugal?'

I make a calculation. Nora is Irish. If at first I say no, she'll think I really mean yes. If I say yes, she'll also think I really mean yes. In other words, I can't get out of having a frugal.

'I'd love one. Thanks.'

Nora smiles again, gets up and goes into the kitchen.

Old Ira continues with his story.

'Where was I? Oh yeh. Momma was worried. Herschel, there's no future in frugals, what'll we do with our boy? There's no life for him here in this one ox shtetl.'

Nora returns with a frugal. She places the plate in front of me. A frugal is alarmingly big. It looks like a cooked fez without a tassel. I dig in. I smile approvingly as I attempt to swallow a particularly hard piece of indeterminate cooking ingredient. I clear my throat and continue with my questions.

'So everyone back in Ireland would wonder how this Jewish boy from Pogromia ended up in the GPO in 1916?'

'Bad luck. Poppa had a distant cousin in Hollywood, had become a big-shot film producer, Manfred Members, Mannie Members he was known as, he sends me a telegram. I was over the moon.'

'Anyone would be.'

'But we were uneducated people. People talk about the Jews and their love of books and learning, that's a load of bupkiss, there were a lot of stupid Jews out there including myself, my momma and my poppa. Stupid Jews! None of us knew where this Hollywood place was. I got my hands on an atlas. There's two Hollywoods' listed. One with two 'l's' in California. One with one 'l' in County Down in this place called Ireland.'

I nod and try chewing some more. I realize the frugal is an acquired taste I have yet to acquire. Ira is lost in the past.

'Of course, it was the fault of the telegram girl back in California. She couldn't spell. I re-read the telegram. 'Ira, come to Holywood, I'll make you a big star, I'll put you in the great silent film director D.W. Griffith's new epic sensation *The Birth of a Nation*. That illiterate telegram girl changed the course of my life.'

'So you find yourself in County Down?'

'Yeh. I get a ferry from Hamburg to Larne late April 1916. It was a very bumpy ride, the boat kept hitting off the tops of those U-boats on the way over, what with The Great War going on. The Great War. What kind of term is that? As opposed to, what, the Not-So-Great-War? The Ho-hum War? Where was I? Oh, yeh, yeh, it was mayhem with this war. I got off the boat, got on a train to Holywood. I disembark at the train station, but no one is there to greet me. No studio heads. No photographers. No starlets. I am crestfallen. I walk down the platform and suddenly I'm approached by a short man in a long overcoat. The man turns to me and says in a West Belfast accent, 'Are you here for the shooting?' I perk up. 'Yes, 'The Birth of a Nation'?' 'Absolutely! Up the Republic! Follow me!' So I follow the man and before I know it I'm in some post office being shot at, next to this guy Padraig Pearse.'

'What was Padraig Pearse like?'

'A schlemiel. Not a leader of men. The month before the Rising he'd been working in a restaurant, because his school was running up debts, but he got the sack because he kept switching the orders.'

Nora frowns. I sense tension in the air. I also sense a molar being loosened by a piece of frugal. Old Ira looks at me.

'She won't have me say a bad word against him. She idolizes the klutz.'

'He died for Ireland, darling. No greater sacrifice.'

'I'll be honest. I wasn't crazy about dying for Ireland that week. Or being injured for Ireland. Or even being grazed on the knee for Ireland. I was just another wrong-guy-in-the-wrong-place. I kept a low profile most of the time hiding under a table in the telegram girls' room.'

'Do you remember any of the others?'

'The O'Rahilly. On my frequent visits to the whatever, latrine, I kept bumping into this guy called The O'Rahilly. His name fascinated me. But considering he was the only man I ever knew who had a definite article as a forename he was a strangely unremarkable person. Then there was Joseph Mary Plunkett. A true schlimazel. Nothing worked out for him. Every time he tried loading a gun it would just go off in the ceiling and the others would just shout 'Jesus, Mary and Joseph, Joseph Mary, will you ever put that gun away'!"

He yawns at the reminiscing. A lull descends. I spot a picture of a 1930s pin-up on the wall. The picture is signed 'To Yitzhak from Roxie. With all my love, you big lug!'

Old Ira perks up. He has a gleam in his eye.

'Guess who the shiksa is?'

I shrug my shoulders. And stare down with trepidation at the remaining large piece of frugal on my plate. I go to pick it up. Old Ira grins. He points at Nora.

'Nora?'

Nora giggles.

'Sure, wasn't I young once? And like all cailíns I wanted a bit of adventure. I was tired of dancing at the crossroads back in the old country. It was also becoming increasingly treacherous with the onset of the automobile.'

She starts to tell me about her life in Chicago in the early 1930s.

'I had a sister there. Novena. But I was different from Novena. I wanted to break out. Express myself. I became an exotic dancer and started calling myself Roxie Fifi DuPont.'

'The Irish Mata Hari they used to call her,' Old Ira croaks up. 'She was a vixen. Men became putty. Putty! She had so many suitors. Can you imagine?'

Nora adds to the reminiscing.

'In temperament they all said I was a cross between Mae West and Greta Garbo. A gentleman caller would ring me and I'd say 'Come on up and see me'. When he'd arrive at my place, I'd tell him 'Go away, I want to be alone.'

'In looks too!' Ira interjects. 'The profile of a Garbo but the tuchus of a West!'

I suddenly imagine I'm with one of those old couples that appear intermittently throughout the film *When Harry Met Sally* recollecting how they met. A warm nostalgic glow envelopes the room. I subtly move the plate with the frugal to the edge of the table. But too far. It falls off. The plate breaks as a piece of moonrock hits the carpet. There is silence. Is Nora from Noraid pondering whether a kneecapping is too good for me? No. She too is lost in memory. She gestures she'll tidy it later as she starts talking about their courtship.

'Ira had finally ended up in America. His cousin Yitzhak was in Chicago and he'd been one of my suitors but when I first saw Ira with his sweet wrong-guy-in-the-wrong-place-look I fell hook, line and sinker, buster!'

There was one final complication though. A spat over spats. Nora continues.

'Yitzhak and Ira shared an apartment. I'd stopped seeing Yitzhak but had started seeing Ira. Ira's birthday was coming up. I bought him a pair of spats as a present. But when Yitzhak got home early he recognized my writing on the card and thought the spats were for him. I had to come around to the apartment and explain about the spats. The funny thing is Ira was baffled by the gift and just wanted to know why people wore spats. This spat over the spats lasted the whole evening. And into much of the next day. But it brought Ira and myself even closer together.'

Nora blushes. Old Ira slowly lifts up the bottom of his trousers. His sticklike legs are each covered, below the knee, by a strange black & white piece of cloth.

'These are those exact pair of spats. Wouldn't go a day

without wearing them. And for old people they are great for the circulation.'

Old Ira and Nora smile at each other and slowly grab hold of each other's hand.

I take my leave of one of the happiest couples I've ever met and as I dwell upon early 20th century nationalism, dead Irish heroes, Chicago of the 1930s, and the longevity of love, there's a lightness in my heart, a briskness in my step and a meteorite-sized lump in my stomach.

* Because it was submitted a day after the closing date for submissions, 'Memoirs of an Unlikely Rebel' was not considered for the Lidl Short Story of The Year Award. The fifty euro entry fee was forfeited.

THE END